THE LATEST BLOODSHED

THE LATEST BLOODSHED

Jim Stallings

iUniverse, Inc.
New York Lincoln Shanghai

The Latest Bloodshed

iUniverse books may be ordered through booksellers or by contacting:

iUniverse
2021 Pine Lake Road, Suite 100
Lincoln, NE 68512
www.iuniverse.com
1-800-Authors (1-800-288-4677)

ISBN-13: 978-0-595-36363-6 (pbk)
ISBN-13: 978-0-595-67371-1 (cloth)
ISBN-13: 978-0-595-80800-7 (ebk)
ISBN-10: 0-595-36363-6 (pbk)
ISBN-10: 0-595-67371-6 (cloth)
ISBN-10: 0-595-80800-X (ebk)

Printed in the United States of America

For Clans Stallings, Lewis, Baker & Strickland
&
Their Art of Southern Storytelling
&
Especially for my Mother
Millie Velma Baker

A tender heart that hates non-being, vast and black
Assembles every glowing vestige of the past!
The sun is drowning in its dark, congealing blood...
In me your memory, as in a monstrance, shines!

—#47. The Harmony of Evening
The Flowers of Evil
Charles Baudelaire

...Then the Lord put a mark on Cain so that no one who found
him would kill him. So Cain went out from the Lord's presence
and lived in the land of Nod, east of Eden.

—*Genesis* 4: 15-16

"On the Cross between Heaven and these Blues..."

—"How Great Thou Art"
Old Gospel Song

CHAPTER 1

▼

Was it raining? It didn't matter. At some point in all his dreams, Jelly Lovejoy knew it had to rain. Trouble had to come home to roost. That was the nature of where he was. Strickland County, Georgia, county seat, Warden. Forty thousand souls in the Land of Nod. This was Jesus country. Old and New Testament. A hard land laced with blood and suffering. And in his recurrent nightmare, there was something dark and cloudy, plasma of sorts, nothing definite, except in flashes it took on definiteness, yes it did…and it chased him through his dreams. Like down a slick silver highway through the dark Georgia night. And there was that rain, making things slick. Like blood…slick and sticky all at the same time. And if you made the wrong move, you'd be off that road and off into the pine forest night. And then God help you, nobody knew for sure the limits of your suffering. It took Jelly a long time to figure out what it was chasing him through the dark nights. But it was akin to ignorance. Bilious, unformed, never certain, never obvious, just a vague display of horrid ignorance. One hand not knowing the other…

And it came after you like a mob of monsters that could not get enough of hate and pain. They wanted to punish Jerry "Jelly" Lovejoy for all his wandering thoughts. What had he been thinking when he first began to question things? Was he insane?

But there it was, that questioning mind, asking, does it have to be this way? And the answer from the rearview mirror was, yeah, boy, it does have to be hard and mean and stupid. This is the land of suffering…and the dark hostile force redoubled and chased his failing car through the Georgia nights and he stuck his head out into the wet and cried out for a savior and he or she just didn't come…That cruelty behind him, Death, or whatever it was, just came on apace and swallowed him…

And he awoke in a sweat in his great aunt's old farm house where he now lived alone and he howled. He howled his pain and shook the heartwood old frame that sustained him above the alluvial clay soil of Strickland County, miles only from the Florida line. These semi-tropical fantasies with all its rich farm lands alight with the ghosts of the past. Jelly screamed his pain, his absolute fear, and shook in a malarial sweat 'til he pitched back into his wet sheets and stared once again at the speckled ceiling of his family's old homestead. You boy, somebody whispered, you got the curse of remembering. The ghosts of the ancestors walked the soil all around him and he knew in his gut he couldn't escape their curses.

"I'm not carrying this guilt anymore," he said to no one in particular and rose to drench his head in a sink of cold well water. In the kitchen window's reflection he saw a tall young muscled man with wild blonde hair, slumped forward, his face freckled by years in the sun…his wide set gray eyes sunken in dark shadows of fatigue.

Overhead a lonely pilot ferried a tiny plane through the dark moonless night. The drone of the engine gave him some sense of his own time but the past in all its thickness came round him like a suffocation, an asthma of gasping breath that caused him to see stars in the black hallway of the old frame farmhouse. Sleep, sleep, he whispered, and made his way back to his bed and slumped back into the damp cotton.

God help me, he prayed, and felt himself sinking into the great miasma of dreams and fears again. Soon, too soon, his own present life would be awakening with the morning sun. He had to outrun that reality, he had to make his way through the darkness to that light where he had a chance to vanquish the weight of the past.

Coyotes yipped in the woods to the east. A hoot owl called out of the ramshackle old tobacco curing barn, put together with pegs and dowels, now leaning over at a crazy angle, all the past shading its weariness into his present life. Was this fair? It didn't matter. It was the truth. He gasped for breath and in his exhaustion, in his battle with ignorance and death, and every other unknown, fell backwards into blessed dreamless sleep.

CHAPTER 2

▼

Chief Eldridge stopped Jelly outside the briefing room.

"How long you been a detective?" he asked, his gray eyebrows flying in a wild disarray as if he'd seen too much in his forty years on the force.

"Finishing my first year next month."

"You look like hell. Circles under your eyes. What's up with you?"

"I'm trying to make up my mind about the law. You know, go back to school and take a law degree."

"You studied criminology and social work, right?"

"Yes sir, you know my background."

"Yes I do, Detective Lovejoy. I know you're a bleedin' heart for the underdog. You'd make a great public defender. So what's so hard about that making the commitment…You must be torn up about something."

"I like my police work but I keep wondering if there's something else I should do while there's still time."

"While there's still time?" The Chief regarded him, tapping his briefing papers. "I'd hate to lose you, that's for sure. But I've seen burnout before, Love-joy, and I'd say there's more to this than a professional career decision. Maybe there's a woman. Or something you can't talk about."

Jelly gave him a hard look. What the hell was he driving at? Sure there was a woman. Connie Sorensen. He'd been dating her off and on steadily for years. But as yet neither of them was ready to make the commitment.

"That cute little nurse you go with," the Chief smiled, his jowls shaking like a hound dog sniffing out a cold case. "Just tell me when I'm too nosy."

"You're there, Chief," Jelly said. "You got nothing to worry about. I'm good to go."

"Yeah. How much vacation time you got built up?"

"I don't know. I take off a day here and there to go fishing and just hang out with my thoughts."

"Uh huh, I've never learned much from fish. Anyway, after this next drug sweep goes down…I want you on a two week leave."

"Oh, come on Chief."

"That's an order. You got the hundred yard stare, buddy. Combat fatigue."

Godammit! Jelly went out to his county-issued gray Buick sedan and slumped into the front seat. He had a list of people to see, cases to investigate and he just didn't need this kind of intrusive psychobabble horseshit from the Chief. Overhead the clouds of November were running low, thick air from the Gulf moving up from the Panhandle of Florida. A hurricane warning in effect for later in the week. Light rain spattered his windshield as he pulled out of the garage and entered the side street next to the new consolidated city and county police station.

Downtown on the square the beautiful old white courthouse with its four sides of dark tall windows and its varnished old wood interiors echoing with footsteps called his name. Courthouse lawyer. So much history had passed through those doors and trial rooms. Every known human tragedy had entered the dusty county books over the past century and a half. And his family the Lovejoys and his mother's family, the Russell's, had been an active part of that. He sat at the light and stared at the clock on the north side of the courthouse, nearby the Confederate soldier statue stood at attention, a dun color in the morning rain.

There came a tapping at his passenger side window. Snake Roberts' greasy face loomed in the beaded glass. Jelly ran down the window and eased over to the curb. Jelly had known him since elementary school.

"What's up, Snake?"

"Gimme a lift out to Sunnyside Projects, Jelly."

"Get in…"

Snake slid into the seat and let out a deep breath and shook himself.

Jelly smelled alcohol and something else off his skin and clothes…the faint whiff of crystal meth and body sweat. He was picking at his forearms, jumpy. Their eyes met and Snake looked away.

"I ain't looking for no lecture, Jelly."

"Would it do any good?"

"Fuck no. I'm a mess. This shit's eating me alive. Like a green grasshopper with a red asshole."

"Maybe a walk in the rain would do you good."

"Listen, screw that…I gotta a tip for you. I hear there's reward money."

"Go on," Jelly said, lapping the courthouse square to get lined up for the road southwest to the Sunnyside subsidized housing projects. Now there was a nest of petty criminals feeding off each other.

"These landscapers hauling in semis filled with pine straw…sometimes they're packing in drugs down the center aisle."

"Nothing new there, Snake. Tilt. Try again."

"Okay, Sherlock, think I know who's been stealing meat from Kramer's Market."

"Oh yeah, somebody hungry I hope."

"Don't make no matter does it? Still a damned crime, ain't it?"

"By the book, yep, for sure."

"You going soft, boy?"

"Snake, do I look like Robin Hood?"

"No, not with that badge and that thirty-eight on your hip."

"So let's do the right thing."

"Handel brothers. Wise ass niggers. Been selling steaks off their truck on the highway near the Farmer's Market."

"Terry and Matt's boiled peanut stand?"

"Honest to God, you got that right. They keep the meat iced down in a Styrofoam cooler in the cab of the truck."

"You see that with your own eyes?"

"Well, my old lady did. She come a runnin' to tell me."

"Maybe she deserves the reward."

"Oh, she'll get her fair share. You can count on that."

"She still cooking up that bathtub meth?"

Snake shook involuntarily and pointed at Jelly. "You're the wise guy, eh? You know I fucked off that shit. It'll eat your goddamned brains up. I can't afford to lose more gray matter, Jelly. You know that."

"There's word out there's a shortage of quality crystal meth in the county since we last did a sweep."

"I ain't fuckin' with those assholes. They're crazy motherfuckers."

Jelly let the car glide through the light gray rain and pulled to the entrance to Sunnyside Housing.

"You probably don't want to be seen with me, Snake."

"That's for sure. There's eyes all over this pisshole project. Lips gone aflappin..."

Jelly waited. Snake clawed at the back of his left hand. Sure enough sign of the lye of cheap meth working its way through his skin. Poor sonofabitch. He looked sixty but he knew they were the same age.

"So, uh, anything in this for me," Snake said.

"Yeah, I'll buy you a bag," Jelly said.

"A bag of what?"

"Bag of boiled peanuts."

"Fuck you," he grinned. "Come on, man, can you advance me a little on the reward? You know, money, honey. Let's dance, eh?"

"If it pans out, you'll get the reward from Kramer's. Hundred bucks."

"Shit I sure could use something now," Snake said, hanging in the half open door, his lower lip drooping, a cotton boll of spittle stuck there.

Jelly stared at him hard and opened his wallet and flipped him a twenty.

Snake snatched it up. "Well, guess I can trust you for the rest, seeing how we're old school buddies."

"Two-way street now, Snake. We're supposed to be grown-ups. School days, that's a long time in the rear view. Thanks for the tip."

"Any other research you need?"

Jelly looked at him like down a telescope reversed in time. "Tell me, Snake, why's everybody in this country so strung out on something?"

"Shit, ain't it obvious, college boy, we're all fucking bored!"

Jelly just stared at him trying to grasp the horror of that vast boredom.

Snake grinned big, his top teeth missing, the twenty balled up in his claw-like hand. "You have yourself a nice day, Officer Lovejoy."

Snake eased down in the ragged sofa in his basement apartment and lit the pipe and sucked up the smoke. He coughed and kept on coughing and then started gagging.

"Godammit!" he cursed and spat into the corner of the living room, dark now with only light in the back bedroom and a wan light from the rainy day outside in Sunnyside Acres. "Where's that bitch anyway?"

He sucked at the pipe again and went through the same routine, coughing up phlegm and swallowing. He put the crude pipe down.

"Just shit, fuckin' low down crap," he gurgled and threw his head back on the sofa. He heard a key in the door and it opened slightly.

"Who's in there," came a meek voice.

"Who the hell you think?" Snake said and saw his gal friend's sallow worn face. Man, she'd aged like a sonofabitch this past year. Her hair was falling out and her skin was yellow parchment. She looked like some old witch creeping into a bad movie on cable TV…which reminded him he wanted to watch that movie tonight about the bloodsucking vampires and the werewolves that ate children for their fresh livers. Some shit like that…

"It's you, Snake," the woman said and eased the door shut.

"Lock it for god's sake, Kelly, ain't you got good sense. You think we're living with honest people?"

She laughed and muttered something.

"Don't be fuckin' muttering under ya breath at me. Speak the fuck up."

"You score some crystal?"

"Hell no. Cops everywhere around town. I tell you there's something heavy coming down. Another raid. We better lay low and use what we got of the cheap shit you bought."

"It's aggravating me something awful," she said and stepped closer to him across the broken-legged coffee table.

"You look like shit."

"I know it but I gotta get high to shake this. I can't go cold turkey. I'll have to go into the hospital."

"You ain't going into that treatment program again and spilling your guts. No wonder the cops are always watching us."

"Did you speak with that detective friend of yours?"

"Yeah, I tipped him on the Kramer meat deal. He wouldn't pay me nothing in advance, that bastard. Cheap shit went to school with me. He knows I ain't never had a damn thing, nary a break."

Kelly sat down on the front edge of a folding chair and began wringing her hands and moaning softly.

"Oh shut your hole, will ya?"

"I ain't feeling good, Snake. I'm feelin' real bad. Real bad."

Snake leaned forward and hung his head and stared at the dark brown rug. Something small was crawling through the worn tufts. Jesus, he thought, I'm living in filth and that Jelly is cruising around the county like a goddamned big shot gun slinger. He was tougher than that pussy cop. What the fuck kind of world was this?

Kelly started her moaning again.

"Here, smoke some of this bathtub scum," he said and shoved the ceramic pipe under her nose.

Kelly began to gag, slowly, convulsing and twitching in her torso. Her head snapped back and her face looked like she'd had a stroke.

"Please, Snake, you gotta help me."

"Fuck it, woman, here!" He snatched out the twenty and pushed into her face. She gripped it next to her nose and sniffed it.

"Oh, thank you, Jesus!" she cried and sank to her knees. "A Jackson."

Snake grabbed her up and shoved her toward the door. "Promise'm anything. Tell'em it's an advance on a deal in the makin'…just don't come back without some of the quality shit."

"This won't buy much."

He shoved her out the door and pointed at her shrunken wrinkled living cadaver. "Don't come back without some and don't use it before coming home."

"Don't be mean, Snake, it's Friday. We can party."

"Yeah, Friday night when the eagle flies, sweetheart. Now, git!"

CHAPTER 3

▼

Just beyond the WalMart plaza and the County Hospital, Jelly spotted the Handel's setup on the side of the highway. The wind was blowing and cars blasting by on the wet pavement shook the canopy over the cart and blurred it with the wave of spray. Jelly slowed and pulled off the road on the shoulder. He only spotted one man behind the makeshift wagon. The younger of the Handel's...Matt. He was adjusting the flame under the bucket of boiling salt water.

"Hey, if ain't Officer Lovejoy." He grinned and his big black face lit up. His clothes were damp and he rubbed his hands over the fire.

"This gotta be a tough day for sales," Jelly said.

"Gotta fight the man," Matt said. "WalMart over there...all those big chains, they can't make'm like we local folk know how."

"That's for sure," Jelly said. "I saw some for sale the other day in an aluminum kind of bag. I thought, this can't taste good and when I saw the price...three or four bucks I think it was...I knew then, I gotta keep tradin' local."

Jelly shook Matt's strong hand. "Good to see you, man. How's everything?"

Matt had been a great halfback on the high school football team. Hundred yard games were normal for him. School work wasn't. He was frequently unemployed. A man with an attitude, according to his employers who called the Sheriff to complain and file dire warnings. But there hadn't been anything serious. A little dope dealing maybe. One case of selling ecstasy to high school kids that had formed a sex club. But that was before Matt and his older brother Terry had found wives and started families. The meat heist made sense as food and cash flow.

Matt handed Jelly a small brown paper bag of boiled peanuts. "On the house, my man."

"Can't do that," Jelly said. "Against the practices now."

Jelly handed him a dollar and Matt took it.

"Man, things are getting down right righteous since we were kids. I remember my daddy giving old man Foster a buck or two to keep him off our asses."

Jelly squeezed the wet, warm peanut and swallowed the salty juice and chewed them into a gray paste. "Damn good, Matt."

"That reminds me," Matt said, "You're no flatfoot now. You're a detective. I see you in those khakis and blazer and that orange shirt with the blue seal. I say, my oh my, what have I done now? That's a plainclothes cop. But that's old Jelly…so congratulations."

"Thanks, Matt."

Jelly smiled and walked around the cart. He didn't see a Styrofoam cooler. A semi blew by them rocking everything with a wet blast of road spray.

"Guess you know why I'm stopping by?" Jelly said and squared around on Matt.

"We ain't peddling dope."

"How 'bout stolen meat?"

Matt adjusted the flame under the big can of salt water, the steam pouring off, the earthy smell of peanuts churning. Matt laughed.

"This about that Kramer market break-in?"

"Yep."

"Shit, I wish! I'd love to be eating sirloin and filet mignon. Training table food. That's the kind of meat they get up at Georgia. You know I almost got to Georgia on football scholarship?"

"I heard about that. What happened?"

"Grades. I can't read good. Dyslexia…the letters jump around on me."

"Sorry about that."

"Life's a bitch, ain't it, but what you gonna do?"

"Where's Terry?"

"He had to run into town and get some things."

"Be back soon?"

"Hard to say," Matt said and laughed. "He leaves me out here half the day sometime."

"Doesn't seem fair."

"Yeah, but I do it to him when it's my turn."

"Well, I'd like to talk to him and see if he's heard anything. You know there's a hundred dollar reward for info leading to a conviction."

"Nope, didn't know that," Matt said and lit a cigarette. "You want one, Jelly?"

"I'll pass."

Matt puffed on his cigarette and the acrid smoke swept up into the peanut steam cloud. Jelly noticed he had a cell phone bulge in his shirt jacket. That meant there'd likely be a call to Terry the minute he left.

"You know, Jelly, things ain't going good for a lot of folks around here."

Jelly nodded in assent. "It's rough all over."

"Just these shitty minimum wage jobs. Part time, no health care. You know my woman Juanita, she's got fibroids, been bleeding a lot. She lost a baby last fall. Been depressed. My Mama's gettin' on and she's got that Alzheimer stuff. We gotta watch her night and day."

"I'm seeing that everywhere," Jelly said, thinking of his Grandma Rose in her nineties. "I'm real sorry."

"And Terry's youngest kid, Amos, he got hurt in a car wreck. No insurance. Hell, he's gonna be broke for the rest of his life payin' that off."

Jelly cocked his head. "You trying to tell me something, Matt?"

"Not exactly…"

"Help me out here," Jelly said and handed him two more dollar bills and received two more bags of peanuts. "Need some for my Mama and Daddy out at the farm."

"Sure enough," Matt said and stuffed the dollar bills into a Hav-A-Tampa gold cigar box.

"So, what's going on, Matt?"

"Honest to God, Jelly, I ain't a player…but you know there's something going on in Strickland County and its coming this way soon. The Mexicans. The dope coming in from Texas. You sure know about that?"

"We've got a pretty good idea, but if you know something that could help that would be good."

Matt looked around as several passing cars overcame his voice. "The old-timers say it's in all the signs…the Ax Man coming back. There's gonna be a killin' time. That's on the gossip line. The Mexicans and whites…a war over the drugs…especially over the speed trade. The Mexicans want to take away the speed market from the red necks."

"What's the Black attitude toward this?" Jelly said.

"Smoke a little weed and cool the fuck out!" Matt said and laughed deep and hard. "We ain't gettin' into the hard drug thing. All our charm readers are seeing it in the cards…the Ax Man is coming…he's coming again…honest to God, that's the low down from the quarter. There's gonna be blood and lots of it. It's like a boil about to burst."

"Does it always have to be like that?" Jelly mused.

"Hell, man, life in Warden's like watching tropical fish in a tank. Everybody seems quiet and getting along, you know, and then wham…one fish attacks another in a frenzy and it spreads and somebody's dead, floating belly up…quick as the eye all the different kinds of fish just swimming around like nothing every happened."

"Maybe that's what's fascinating about fishing?" Jelly said.

Matt smiled. "Now there's a thought for the day."

Matt punched up his brother Terry on the cell. There was static and noise from the friggin' highway.

"Hey, who's this?" Terry said, sleepily.

"Matt, your sore ass brother left out here to rot."

"Cool it out, son," Terry came back, laughing low. "I'll be out there in a minute and we can switch off?"

"Guess who was here?"

"How the fuck should I know," Terry said. "Snow White and the Seven Dwarfs?"

"The fuzz, bro. Jelly Lovejoy, Officer Detective Lovejoy."

There was silence on the other end, then a curse Matt couldn't make out.

"So, what's he want?" his older brother said, sounding heavy and sad.

"Better not talk too much. No telling what's being scanned."

"Well, you're right there, and there's nothing we done."

"That's right but he was asking about that Kramer meat market break-in and word being maybe we was selling it."

"Hell, if we had that meat, we'd eat it first. Was he pushing hard?"

"No, just poking around with a tip, I guess."

A panel truck with charcoal black windows cruised close by and slower than normal and Matt couldn't make out the driver's face.

"I'll be out there in a little bit. You just sit tight and sell the hell outta them boiled peanuts. I got a little errand to run."

"I thought you might," Matt said. "I'd say we'd need some more raw peanuts to boil too."

"Roger on that, goober," Terry said and laughed. "Well, sorry I missed Detective Lovejoy. I guess he's moved on…"

"Oh yeah, said something about visiting his grandma and giving her some boiled peanuts."

"Well, it's just old home week, ain't it?" Terry said. "Too bad I missed him."

"Yeah, it's all in the timin', nigger."

Terry laughed. "Yeah, I always was shufflin' late for the man…thank you Jesus for that."

CHAPTER 4

▼

"Grandma," Jelly called out, knocking firmly on the trailer door.

They'd moved her to this small one bedroom rig after her old farmhouse got too much for her. The old place stood under a copse of shaggy pecan trees. Her local paper, the *Warden City Times,* was in the bushes. Jelly picked it up and noted the picture of the new Catholic priest in town, brought in from Texas, a Father Diego Rodriguez, to handle the Masses in Spanish for the growing Mexican fieldworker population. He looked like a round-faced boy.

Jelly repeated his call and knock. He heard movement from the rear.

"Who's that?" came a feeble voice, a bit nervous it seemed to him.

"It's Jelly, Grandma, I stopped by for a visit."

"Who'd you say?"

"Jelly! Your grandson."

He saw the curtain pull aside and a pale face slip past toward the door. "Just a minute, Sam."

Sam was Jelly's grandpa, dead some twenty years. The door swung open and Jelly smiled at his Grandmother. She was ninety something. And despite a bit of confusion about who was who in the present, her old memories were frequently and lucidly intact.

"Come on in, honey," she said and waved toward the little built-in kitchen. "I was just making some oatmeal and coffee."

Jelly hugged her and felt her tiny bones inside the big housecoat. She rarely got dressed anymore. A public health nurse visited her daily.

"Miss Draper come by yet?" Jelly asked.

"Who?"

"Your nurse. Miss Draper."

She smiled sweet as she could be. "You're not Sam, are you? I just figured you were Sam come back from plowing. Still early, I thought. I didn't have a thing ready for lunch. Well, maybe something happened with that old tractor of yours."

"It's me, Jelly, your grandson."

She laughed. "I can see that now," she said and squinted. "You sit down and I'll fix you something."

There was nothing on the stove. They'd had to disconnect the gas. She left it on and once caught her sleeve on fire. His Mama and Daddy he knew had threatened to move her into their extra room on the back of their house or else commit her to a nursing home. I'm dyin' right here, she had said, before you take me away from the farm.

"Can't stay long," Jelly said and pushed some clothes aside on the sofa and found a seat. "I brought you some boiled peanuts. Fresh boiled."

"Oh, ain't you sweet now," she said and reached out her gnarled arthritic fingers to take the paper bag. "Where'd you get these?"

"Off of Matt Handel over on the Florida road near the hospital."

"Matt Handel," she said, sucking the first one down with a raspy breath. "Uh huh, that's good, not too much salt. I'm sure glad you brung me these cause I misplaced my teeth and I sure don't need nothing but gums to mash these juicy things up. The Handels...that's a nigger family, ain't it?"

"Yep, they're black folks, Grandma."

"I used to have a woman cook for me named Handel years back."

"That was their great aunt...Jane."

"That's her...She was a good woman. Hard working, boy, let me tell you and she had a passel of her own too. Wonder what come of her..."

Grandma Rose sat in her rocker and sucked and chewed a few more peanuts. It grew quiet in the trailer and Jelly shifted his weight on the sofa and spoke softly, even so causing her to jerk out of her reverie.

"Matt Handel mentioned something," Jelly said, "something about the Ax Man."

"Matt who?"

"The Handels...Matt and Terry, brothers..."

"Don't know them, honey, but maybe Sam does."

Jelly smiled. "You remember those stories about the Ax Man, don't you?"

She sucked on a peanut, draining the liquid, gumming the gray paste, tasting it, her foggy cataract eyes circling the room.

"Not much to say on that, honey. Just a bunch of lies. Nigger lies."

"What do you mean?"

"After them lynchings way back, that old Edwards boy, Tommy was his name, he was de-formed you know, making him a white giant. He got it in his head to get revenge on everybody. Went over to the prison warden's house and took their ax out back where they killed chickens and he went up to the back door and he invited his big self right into their little kitchen and he just chopped up the warden and his wife. Left the pieces right on the kitchen table. Some say he cooked up his favorite parts and ate'm. Sure enough…boy was a cannibal and you know he had webbed feet."

"I've heard that."

She squinted at Jelly and smiled. "And that ain't all."

"What else?"

"He kept comin' back doing his so-called justice for all them lynched niggers and he was a white boy…although folks around Strickland County began to doubt that. Sam said he'd shoot him dead if he ever crept up on our property. All them niggers in town made him out to be a hero! I know for sure he used to camp out at the old lime sinks around the county."

"How 'bout the one on Grandpa's farm?"

"Oh sure, we found his tracks. Big webbed feet. When the sink was filled with water, then you'd see him lurking around. He knew better than to come up to my door for a biscuit. Blood thirsty monster."

"He'd be dead by now, don't you think?" Jelly said. "I mean that was, what, seventy years ago, wasn't it?"

"I was fresh married when he killed that judge. It weren't right what them Klan fools did to those niggers over in Jarvis. They claimed those young bucks was gettin' uppity and talkin' 'bout starting something with the white women. I'll tell you this, I never had a colored man disrespect me. But you know these jealous white men. Oh, they got their dander up and went over there and shot'em up and hung'em. They burned one old boy. It was mean and not a Christian thing to do."

"No ma'am," Jelly said and stared out the window at the pine trees thick through the woods to the county dirt road. "That's a sad story for so-called Christians to remember."

"My grandfather Tate was still alive and he preached a mighty sermon against them men. You know they burned a cross on his yard and called him a nigger lover. He died not long after that. Those bastards got off with a little sentence and the town went crazy up at the courthouse. Sam took me home in the old truck and just about burned it up gettin' out here away from the craziness."

"Then the Ax Man, Tommy Edwards, sought justice?"

"He sure did. He chopped up the judge and his wife and then he killed most of them Klansmen he sure did. It took him a while but he tracked them down and split'em down the middle like kindlin' wood. He'd put their heads on fence posts. Birds pecked out their eyes. Old Doctor Trellis told me the Ax Man ate their hearts and livers. I never was sure about that. Old Doc kinda spread it thick now and then…I think he liked to scare us young women. He sure done that…"

"They never found the Ax Man, did they?"

"No sir, they found his lair, and his axes and knives…and a heap of skulls and bones…but nary a hide nor hair of that monster."

"Gotta be dead by now," Jelly said.

"Who told you that?"

"Nobody."

"He ain't dead, son, he's just laying back 'til the next revenge time. You mark my word."

"Matt Handel said the Blacks in town are saying he's coming back now. There's gonna be bloodshed over all the drug trade going on."

"Drugs. You don't fool with them drugs, do you?"

"No, Grandma, I'm a cop."

"You are?"

"Yep, ten years now."

"Oh, that's right. Sam and I are mighty proud of you."

"Thanks."

"Yeah, that old monster Ax Man…he be coming back…niggers know things like that…that old man is the Devil's right hand man."

She sucked up another wet peanut and massaged the gray goo with her cratered sunken lips. Her eyes watered and she stared in Jelly's direction.

"You be careful, boy, you hear me? Better have eyes in the back of your head."

"I'll be real careful."

She shook her head. "I'm feeling kinda tired now. I best lie down for a while…that nurse is coming out here to bathe me and Sam said to do whatever she said to stay healthy, keep my blood pressure low."

Jelly gave her a hug and helped her to her bed. She stretched out, her wispy white hair blowing under a tiny fan on the wall. Her eyelids quivered and she began to snore gently. Through the milky morning light pearly now with a sheen of sunshine and mist, Jelly imagined for a second he saw a hulking dark figure fading into the palmetto and pine forest.

Ain't no sense in what I done or what I will do. No sir. You think life is something you understand, but take it from me, Tommy Edwards, webbed footed monster, Ax Man haunting your dreams, I am the devil's helper. I bring the bloody justice down on these unshaven guilty heads. The blood drips from everywhere and when it gets thick and deep enough, when it crawls through the cracks of my home down in the lime sinks, then yes sir, it's Tommy Edwards revenge time. And that old woman lying there in her trailer, she knows the truth about me...some anyway, cause she for sure goes back to my time on this earth...alive in every part...and living off this land with butchery in my heart.

The lime sinks pull me under into caves where I float in my weightless suit of ancient flesh, rotten through and through, until the call above comes trickling down. That's the horror of it all and when I was a boy and the people would stare and point, when they whispered 'bout my webbed feet and my mama and daddy being sister and brother, about me being a devil child of incest, they thought I wasn't listening but I was. I always was listening and my ears detected at great distances the cries of the innocent and the snarling of the evil ones. Their eyes flashed in the darkness of night and flickered behind their windshields as they cruised the back roads while I stood in the trees and watched them go about their sick business. Oh, don't deny the truth...that don't get no mercy from an Ax Man. No, my ax splits the body like a log waiting for the fire in winter. The flesh ripping, the skull cracking, the backbone popping like popcorn. The smell of fresh kill and the foul odor of evil from the bad people. The stench is something awful. The innocent...well, that's another story. Their elixir is a delight to the good and bad amongst the devil's helpers.

The times drips with evil blood and seeping down into the ground it awakens me and makes me rise up through the underground rivers, reaching up to the surface of foul stagnant waters of lime sinks deep in old forests...where there I float on my back and smile into the freckled starlight night. These lands of the living...a feast for cannibals of the night...and a purpose driving me to clean house. Oh I remember the catch phrases. I was here once and come again in times of deep need and in my churning heart I feel the dark red ooze calling me to the woodlands and misty valleys and shadowed groves. There's bad things doing again and the times are low and my mission is highly needed. I wander the tracks I know so well from season to season, glancing here and there, taking account of what my nose smells off the so-called innocent of this blood-soaked land.

I hear those gunshots in the distance. I know those boys, those Nesbit boys, or maybe it was their fathers or mothers, grandparents or ancestors way back. But I know that tattoo of killing, those gunshots as familiar as I know those Lovejoys and that Jelly and what he done to his cousin that day down by the pond. No matter what, nobody gets out alive...not even me but some of us, duty bound in our rage, have found a soul-less land that keeps us in need. Like the old woman Rose said to Jelly, better keep an extra pair of eyes in the back of your head...and that goes for all the good citizens of Strickland County....cause I'm back and there's business to do.

CHAPTER 5

▼

Jelly took a slow breath. Fall again. And the damp wet weather. Colder now. Hunting for quail and dove. Deer and turkey. Whatever moved had a bull's eye on it.

There were those shotguns again. Those Nesbit boys. Chop chop chop…Every generation started shooting when they were ten or eleven.

Like his sister Lou Ann said to Jelly last time they went walking in the old growth woods, those Nesbit boys have just about driven off all the animals around here.

Hardly saw a squirrel, certainly the fox squirrel with its long body and tail, stretching across the open; and even the gray squirrel, once plentiful up toward the oak woods, now they were decimated. Jelly considered stopping by their place and reasoning with them. He smiled, they'd likely put a charge in his back and be done with his nosy self. That was one of many a clan that had no respect for the law…only simmering hatred.

Jelly drove up to his folk's house and parked. They'd left the ancestral farm and its difficulties to their oldest, Bill, Jelly's senior sibling. Bill built himself a brick rancher up the road at the corner. He had a few horses and a donkey and kept the acreage in cotton, tobacco and soybeans. Bill was just making it with his wife Celia and their boy and girl, Jay and Tanya, middle schoolers. Bill was in a funk half the time, congenital depression or something, but also down and out over his faith in the farming way of life. Bill hated the idea of selling out and working for somebody in town. On the other hand, his second oldest brother Sammy was a true county seat town citizen and character, with his love of books and magazines and gossip. And Lou Ann, well, there was only one Lou Ann and her comings and goings to Atlanta and Miami. Party girl central. She didn't want to settle down 'til she'd had a run at her dream of being an artist of some kind. Sometimes Jelly believed she knew more about the skuzzy parts of Strickland County and Warden than Jelly did with all his police contacts. When she was in town, unpredictable as the weather, she stayed in a little refurbished sharecropper farmhouse set back on Daddy's remaining farmland, down near the horse pond.

When Jelly thought of the pond, he found he'd stopped walking and was standing by his daddy's old tool barn and his John Deere tractor. He had a blinding flash of pain through his head…wasn't this the anniversary again? That was a doorway that he tried not to pry open more than once a day…but at least that obeisance to guilt and horror made him humble before the potential for violence. A good thing for a man licensed to kill. Simply put, in what had been officially called a hunting accident, he, Jerry Lovejoy, age 12 had without malice aforethought brought his twelve gauge shotgun up quickly to fire at a covey of quail flying up and over a levee of earth holding back a pond wall, and in so doing, in his haste to get a fair shot, had slipped on the muddy embankment, hence causing a sudden drop in the muzzle aim of the aforesaid shotgun and having discharged a shotgun shell at that same moment, the trajectory caught the back of the head of one Henry Parker, age twelve, Jerry Lovejoy's first cousin, at close range causing massive trauma to the skull and brain leading to Henry Parker's almost instant death. As this was an accidental shooting, without malice aforethought, there would be no legal penalties adduced…some such and such in the County of Strickland in the year of our Lord, November 4th, Nineteen hundred and eighty two…and so on and on…

Jelly lowered his head and successfully blocked out the flash of blood and bone normally seen on such daily memorials…just a glimpse but that was enough to tighten his gut and make him want to bend down on the moist crabgrass of his parent's old farmyard and just lay down. Poor old Henry. Poor *young* Henry, rather. If only…if only…a half inch, maybe an inch, would have missed his neck and skull, would have blown by him into the gray moist air. They could have laughed it off and Jelly could have given up hunting right there and then.

Henry was a good kid, wanted to be a doctor like his father and grandfather before him. Had the smarts for it too. He looked up at Jelly and shook his head that last instant before his eyes glazed over. Maybe he was trying to say something but the words didn't come and Jelly was screaming for help. By the time the grown-ups got there Henry was gone.

Last time Jelly saw Lou Ann, a few weeks back, her hair bleached platinum blonde, she shook her curls and said, "How's that Henry Parker thing...how's that really affected you, Jelly?"

And he'd looked at her and said quite bluntly, "What do you think, Lou Ann, it fucked me up for a long time."

"Then you've worked through it, mostly," she said. "It wasn't your fault, Jelly. They shouldn't have let you boys out there without better training."

"Doesn't matter about the excuses. There's no second chance when you kill somebody."

Jelly heard the back door slam on the old farmhouse. He looked up and saw his father squinting at him.

"Hey boy, I told Mama I thought you'd be by...come on in here and we'll catch up on the gossip..."

CHAPTER 6

▼

His Daddy was wearing his Georgia Bulldogs red sweatshirt. He gave a brief bear hug to Jelly. He smelled like wood smoke, sweat and onions and bourbon. He hated bathing on cold days.

"How you feeling?" Jelly said as a practice opening.

"Gonna live 'til I die, son."

"I hear you, Daddy."

"Mighty raw out there today," he said, opening the backdoor. "These damp days make my knees ache. Shrapnel, you know."

"I know," Jelly said, imagining the silvery scars on his father's legs.

Inside the back porch, they passed on through the piles of tools and boxes and disordered gardening pots, where his Daddy hid a pint or two for his arthritis, and passed into the glow of the kitchen. The woodstove was hot enough to broil your face if you came too close. The TV was on and it was blaring the news out of Albany, Georgia. Something about the war on terror and our boys in the Middle East bringing law and order to a chaotic society. A close-up of a dead man in a dusty street was followed by a mortar explosion, then a quick cut to a parade.

"Reminds me of Korea," his Daddy said, his tottering frame bent toward his easy chair. He slid into its blanketed comfort and waved toward the kitchen across the room. "There's your Mama, she's fixing some bacon."

"Hey Mama," Jelly said and stepped into the kitchen, her territory and gave her a hug. She kissed him quickly on the lips and tousled his hair.

She was fussing with the stove. "Hey, honey, I'm just frying up some bacon…how 'bout that and some cheese grits?"

"Oh, I don't know…Mama, I just stopped by for a minute."

"You on duty?"

"Well I'm on call."

"You just sit down here and I'll fix you something."

"All right…just a taste."

"How's that Connie doing? I haven't heard from her in ages."

Connie Sorensen was his old girlfriend, long preferred by the family. A good girl with a medical degree…at least an R.N. degree. His parents liked the idea of smart medical people getting into family. Especially now that they were aging and depending on the doctors and drugs more than ever. They both had a cupful of pills to take each day. His mother's eyesight was blurring with cataracts and whatever else. His dad's joints bothered him and he had heart disease and a tendency toward high blood pressure. The list was endless.

"Oh, Connie and I see each other now and then. She's real busy at the hospital."

"I'm not surprised when you read about all those people shooting and cutting each other," she said and began serving out the food. "Come on Daddy, it's ready."

They sat down together and his Daddy looked down at his plate. "Heavenly Father, forgive us our sins and bless this food to the nourishment of our bodies and us to thy divine service, and amen."

They began to eat with the TV blaring behind them about dish soap and sparkling surfaces, no film, fuss…then a celebrity story about a female rock star who had twins but the father was unknown.

His Daddy looked at Jelly. "I reckon you heard there's a rust outbreak over in Thomas County in the kudzu."

"No, hadn't heard that."

"Yep, damn right, and let me tell you that could wipe out the soybeans in a flash. I been meaning to talk with Bill but he's on one of his fits…"

"Now, Daddy, he's got a lot on his mind," Mama said.

"I told him when he took the farm, I said, Bill, this is getting harder and harder every year to break even. He's no idiot, your brother."

"No sir, Bill's a sharp guy," Jelly said, meaning it. His oldest brother was a stern serious fellow who finished things and suffered no fools.

"Oh, but you listen to Bill now, he's going on about Jefferson and the little two mule farmer and how this country has lost its way. I swear sometimes I wonder if he's gonna make it."

Mama looked at Jelly. "Bill takes after my great grandfather…he was a serious sort. Always taking time off to think things through."

"Yeah, he's out wandering his fields again," Daddy said. "What's that he calls it, that thing they do in Australia?"

"Walkabouts," Jelly said.

His Daddy growled over his grits, "Yeah, he's got his cabbages in and the cotton's done picked and he's out there stomping around miserable 'cause he's facing getting something part-time over the winter. Celia's…she's driving a school bus to help out and working at Sammy's bookstore."

"Well, he's just too proud is what it is," Mama said. "He wants to have them laid back winters like in the old days. Waiting for spring planting. Time for fixing things and doing a little traveling maybe. That poor boy hasn't been on a vacation in twenty years I guess."

"When did you ever go on a vacation?" Jelly teased her.

"Hell's bells," his Daddy said. "We didn't know the meaning of the word. Guess when we went down to Panama City to see our old uncle Lester. That was as close as we ever got to fun in the sun."

Mama laughed. "We did have some good times down there. Even if old Lester was a grump and a drunk."

"He lost a fortune in the stock market back in the Thirties," Daddy said and slurped up his eggs mixed with broken bacon bits. "Man hated to work. My aunt always said he had nigger blood in him."

"That's a lie," Mama said and picked at her food.

Jelly sat for a second and breathed slowly. The heat in the back room was getting to him. He was feeling a little dizzy and dry-mouthed. His Mama glanced at him.

"Honey, you're sweating like a field hand."

"Oh, I'll just get some ice water," he said and went into the kitchen and poured a big glass of water from the fridge.

The TV shouted about Hogan's Heroes re-runs at five every afternoon. A grinning Colonel Klink filled the screen with his joyous pleasure in torturing the American prisoners.

His Daddy turned. "Hell, the chinks in Korea were worse on us. Bamboo under the fingernails. Thank God I wasn't a prisoner of war. I'd a told them anything they wanted to know."

"Oh hush, you would not," Mama said. "You'd have spit in their faces."

His Daddy looked thoughtful. "There was a couple of times when I thought, I just don't care. Let me die. I can't take this cold and wet. That time we were pinned down like bullfrogs in a roadside trench. They was just sniping us to death for two days and two nights. I swear I'd a been glad to be a prisoner about then…but thank god McArthur let loose a tank battalion to get us out. Truman should a let McArthur drop the H bomb on those bastards. You wouldn't have all these problems now. Just postponing the pain. And here's another thing…I tell you I'm tired of pussyfooting with those camel jockeys over in the Near East. Outta take those B-52s and carpet bomb'em back into the desert. Sand people for sure."

Jelly sat down with them again and sipped the cold water. He felt better now. He pretended to watch TV as they finished eating.

His Daddy wiped his lips and tapped him on the arm.

"Got any big busts coming up, son?"

"He can't tell you that," Mama said. "He's warned you about knowing too much, Daddy."

"No, that's okay, Mama," Jelly said. "There's the usual stuff going on…assaults, break-ins, drug use…"

"Them drug busts been quiet for a change," Daddy said. "Them drug cartel boys…that's a group of shit heads that outta be lined up and executed professional style. Bullet through the back of the head. It'd be the Christian thing to do."

"Oh dear, just listen to this man talk," Mama said and brushed back her white hair. "I swear no wonder I need to wear a hearing aid. I could turn that off…"

She laughed and patted Jelly's hand. "You need to eat more. You're looking kind of peak-ed."

"I'll be all right, Mama. I better be going. I gotta check in and see what's what."

"Well, I'm proud of you being on the force, Jelly," she said. "But I worry about those guns and crazy people out there. You be careful now."

He gave them each a hug. His Daddy was already back in his easy chair and was searching for his remote.

Jelly stood at the door and looked at them for a second. His Mama was unloading a bag of green beans on the table. She'd be snapping those in a few minutes while bantering with Daddy.

"Oh, by the way, I stopped over at Grandma's," Jelly announced.

Their two sets of eyes swiveled to a focus on him; they stared at him without comment.

Jelly said, "She was waiting on Miss Draper to come by for her bath and food."

Mama shook her head. "Lord, I need to get over there more often. She won't come over here. Last week she slapped Daddy hard on the face and called him

Sam…Course that was Grandpa's name. She's going fast, Jelly. Her memory's breaking up. Ain't it a shame…"

His Daddy said, "Some days she's like her old self. But there's fewer and fewer of those. She remember you?"

"Thought I was Sam coming home early from the fields. But then she got me right. We talked about the old Ax Man legend."

"The Ax Man!" his Daddy said and slapped the arm of the chair. "That old boy's been dead forty fifty year at least. Ain't she a hoot?"

"Nothing to it," Jelly said. "Just a local legend."

Mama shook her head. "I don't know nothing 'bout no Ax man. My Daddy said that's the devil's talk."

"He was real in his own time," his Daddy said. "But he's just something to keep the niggers worried. Probably making a comeback cause of all these wet-backs…"

Jelly looked at them both. "Well, see you."

"Not if I see you first," his Daddy said and cackled.

His Mama shook her head. "He's an old coot, just ignore him, son."

"I swear, Mama, that boy gives me the creeps sometimes," Jelly's Daddy said and watched out the back window as Jelly climbed into the county car.

"Well, Daddy, he ain't never been the same since he killed his poor cousin Henry. Jelly used to be the happy one in this family of ours. He kept us laughing but that stopped after that."

"Yeah, that'll sober you up right quick. I know it's a lot to bear but for Chrissakes it's been near twenty years. You gotta let go of that stuff and move on. Tell you the truth I think he needed a good war to get rid of that guilt. Ain't nothing like combat to cure you of the fine particulars of murdering folks."

"Oh don't start on that again."

"What you mean? You ain't had to go off to some godforsaken pagan land and shoot people up close. I did."

"I know that. You won't let me forget."

He looked at her and his eyes narrowed. "Well, wait a little longer then 'cause when a man's been through that it's a lifelong song…some of us quieter than others. Me, I don't want nobody to forget…not even a flatfoot son of mine."

"Now that's not polite, he's doing a good job for the folks here in Strickland County. He's a natural policeman. You should hear the nice things ladies at the hairdressers say about…*that Lovejoy boy*…"

"That's just my point," his Daddy said and watched the car fade around the unpaved road over toward Bill's and the old farmlands. He felt an itch to climb in his old Ford pickup and follow but the TV called his attention to a stool softener that might just help with his constipation and then there was a pretty girl in a Bikini beckoning his pecker to a Bahamas casino and clearly it was the devil's work. What would Jesus do? Look away. Condemn it as Sodom and Gomorrah. Well, until that day, it was his job to curl up in front of his glass fronted wood stove and enjoy the fruits of his hard earned labor. Retirement…what a crock of shit but he had to admit it was great fun kissing the weather's ass goodbye. No more praying to the weather gods and making deals with mammon and Wall Street and the Chicago commodity crooks. Piss on all of 'em…

"And that Ax man crap," Daddy called out. "I can't believe a son of mine is runnin' around the county spreading stupid lies from them lazy niggers and wet-backs."

"Now just stop your bad talk and take a nap. I've a house to clean."

"Oh just sit down and take a load off. You'll scrub the last bit of natural wood outta this old chicken shack!"

CHAPTER 7

▼

Bill was forty-five years old now. He'd started to look like Daddy and had the humped shoulders and the bitter attitude toward life. Maybe it was farming, the threat of weather eating at your guts, that bank account always under siege from creditors. But it could be a miserable existence and everybody in the family admired Bill for trying…but Jelly wondered if there wasn't just something stupid and stubborn about Bill's endgame. Two hundred acres wasn't going to cut it anymore.

The mist was now an even light rain and Jelly pulled up in the driveway at Bill's rancher. Celia was in town working at Sammy's bookstore after driving the school bus, so Bill should be about…probably as he had been warned, tromping around the back forty in a blue funk.

But when he came to the side door under the carport, Jelly saw Bill's muddy boots parked on the steps. He must be in the house. He knocked and got no answer. So he went out back and started down toward the barn and out buildings. That's when he spotted Lou Ann's car coming out of the backfield road around the pond. He walked down and opened the gate for her…Bill was in the passenger seat.

"Well, if it ain't the law," Bill said and grinned.

"Hey little brother," Lou Ann called.

"Just out cruising around," Jelly said. "Thought I'd check in. Been a while."

"Come on up to the house," Bill said. "We'll have some coffee."

They sat around the kitchen table. Bill had on the local AM farm station with the soybean prices, Paul Harvey and the latest in traditional country songs. A high-voiced crooner wailed his pain over "Oh Lord, a woman without shame…"

"When you get back from Atlanta?" Jelly asked Lou Ann.

"Late last night. That show of my friend Helen. It was real nice but that mosaic stuff is not my cup of tea. I mean I like it and all, but Jesus, you gotta be a fanatic for every little thing. And transporting those big pieces is hell on wheels, literally."

"What you working on lately?" Jelly asked.

"Those barn paintings…folks like sentimental pictures of the run down farms."

"Shit, listen to that," Bill said. "That's about the size of it too."

Lou Ann was sporting her short, blonde curly look. She had the cute pert face of a comedienne but a bit of hard edge. Jelly always thought of her as a kind of country Doris Day. She was no fool and had been through a lot with men…and he suspected women, although not much was said about the female interests. Unmarried at thirty-four had brought out the suspicion from Sammy, the literary pundit of the family, that indeed our Doris Day was a lipstick lesbian. Jelly didn't mind; didn't think it was his business; police work had made him exclude a lot about people's private lives. He had seen every sort of business behind the facades of so-called ordinary people. In his opinion Lou Ann favored men with Harleys. They were fun but didn't last long.

Bill poured the coffees and put out some Apple crisp Danish.

"I brought the pastries," Lou Ann said. "Got'em at Barrett's this morning. I don't know how they can bake all night and then stand there serving folks all day."

"They don't stay all day," Jelly said. "Their in-laws take over in the afternoons."

Bill laughed. "He's a cop, he outta know what's what with the donuts."

That was the second thing about being a cop. Jelly smiled. He knew it riled Bill that he'd skipped the whole road of farming thing. He'd gone for the city job and gotten a regular check with the promise of a pension. Bill considered that cowardly. Like somebody on the government dole.

"Well, we're creatures of habit," Jelly conceded. "And it gets boring driving around looking for troublemakers."

Bill stirred cream into his coffee. "I bet you guys on the detective side of things don't know half of what goes on in this county."

"That's likely," Jelly said. "We just try to keep a lid on things. Follow the big cases."

"Anything brewing right now?" Bill asked. "It's been kinda quiet so far this fall, hasn't it?"

Lou Ann jumped in. "I don't know about that. I saw where there was a drive by shooting over in Phelps Acres."

"That's the projects," Bill scoffed. "Most of those people are on welfare and got nothing to do but drugs and fuck around with each other."

"It's usually about drugs or money or both," Jelly said. "Sometimes it's about a woman. Payback. That drive-by shooting was likely a turf war over in the Acres."

"And then there's the Mexicans cutting each other up," Bill said. "Some shit always happening over there. I been telling Mama and Daddy to stay put out here in the county. It don't pay to move into town. Too much petty crime, you ask me."

"Yeah, they're happier out here," Jelly agreed. "Just saw them and Grandma on the way here."

"What's this, old home week for you?" Lou Ann asked and tittered, patting his hand. "You feeling sentimental?"

Jelly smiled back at her. He wasn't sure what he was feeling.

"Where's your partner, that black guy, Morris?" Bill said.

"Oh he's on vacation and the chief gave me the day off. I'm on call in case there's a need."

"Rainy Friday," Bill mused. "I'd say the biggest thing will be a knife fight over at Earl's Bar & Grill about midnight."

"And how's things with Connie?" Lou Ann inquired with arched brows. "Are you two ever going to give cohabitation a try?"

Jelly looked from Lou Ann to Bill and shrugged. "Tell you the truth I'm struggling with this whole career thing."

"The law school gig?" Lou Ann said and sipped a spoonful of black coffee.

"Yeah. I'm not sure what I want to do but I gotta make up my mind soon or just give it up."

"Keep your day job," Bill said. "Too many damned lawyers already."

"There is that," Lou Ann agreed. "I'd only do it if I had a real passion for the law. To me that's like taking a knockout drug…pages and pages of fine print." She shuddered. "Gives me the creeps."

Jelly nodded. "There's times when I'm with you on that. Other times I just see it as a way of going beyond the police work. You know, affecting policy, helping to reform the laws."

Bill pounded the table with his fist. He was red-faced. "You want to make a difference. You get out there and save the small farmer. Who's helping us? And don't laugh at me, Lou Ann."

Lou Ann sighed. "You're right, big brother."

"We're not laughing at you, Bill," Jelly said. "We know it's tough."

"Do you? Do you really know what it's like to be down a dark dead end? Two hundred prime acres. I outta sell'em for housing developments. Maybe develop the homes myself. Course I don't know shit about contracting home building but I'm running out of options. Celia's in town everyday working for Sammy, and driving a school bus. You know how that makes me feel."

"I guess it's getting worse," Lou Ann said, sympathetically.

"You're damned right it is," Bill said and tapped the table with his spoon. "You've heard my sermon on this but Tom Jefferson's family farms that do their own labor...that was the American ideal. The yeoman farmer for Chrissake. Now we've got these agro-corps crying they can't compete worldwide without illegal foreigners. That's just a cover up for not wanting to pay American wages and benefits to these wetbacks or us, the leftover white farmers. We're about played out and I bet the Strickland police force doesn't do a damn thing about illegal workers. Right?"

"We do some checking," Jelly said, "but it's at the request of the immigration people."

"Yeah, you're all too busy running around busting penny-anny pot dealers with their nickel and dime bags. You're not helping, Jelly."

"That's my point, Bill, I'm just a foot soldier in this local war. I'm down in the mix of enforcement people. I don't have policy input."

"Policy input," Bill said and pretended to spit. "You bureaucrats are all the same. You got your comfy gig with a hope for pension down the road. You watch the rest of us struggle and die in our own aggravation pits."

"You're not too old to think about something else," Lou Ann said.

Bill stared at her. "I'm thinking about something all right."

"What's that?" Lou Ann said.

"I'm thinking we need to legalize pot. Legalize all the drugs. You realize how much marijuana we could grow on this good bottom land. Slap a government seal on this stuff and let the tobacco companies handle the rest. I'm telling you...it's about the only solution. They say pot is the number two cash crop in a bunch of states...black market of course."

Jelly sipped his coffee and stared out the window toward the rainy woods.

"Well, ain't you going to say anything, Mister Lawman," Bill said and gave Jelly a playful punch in the arm. "You gonna write that up in your report for today?"

Jelly smiled and put down his coffee. "No, I'm not formally on duty and every citizen has a right to express his opinion about the laws of the land. Maybe that's why the law school gambit is appealing to me…sometimes. There's some good arguments to legalizing drugs."

"You better not air that around the station house…they'll think you're some commie fuckin' liberal." Bill pushed back his chair. "I got things to do, folks…Time's a wasting and I can't wait for a lawman hung up on his career path or an artist with pipedreams."

"Hey, don't be so damn mean!" Lou Ann said and looked at Jelly. "He's gettin' as bad as Daddy."

"He is Daddy, you ask me," Jelly said in fun.

Bill mumbled something and left the kitchen and headed down the hall. Lou Ann watched him go and looked at Jelly.

"Guess it's time to go," she said.

"Yeah," Jelly said, "I think the lord of the manor has given us our marching orders."

CHAPTER 8

▼

Outside in the chilly rain Jelly stood next to Lou Ann's blue Malibu and talked to her through her driver side window.

"Honey, you seem like you lost your best hunting dog," she said. "You wanna follow me over to my place and hang out?"

Jelly smiled. He pictured Lou Ann's little refurbished farmhouse. It was nice and cozy and warm but it had too many projects going on everywhere. Piles of canvasses and silver buckets of oil paints and acrylics. Bolts of fabric for her textile cut-outs and her wall designs. Jars of found objects lined the floor and walls, arrowheads, chipped glass, chunks of masonry and china from bygone days. She was an amateur archaeologist of sorts, the kind of artist who could make a beautiful thing out of rusty bailing wire or odd gears from a long ago tractor transmission. Once she had even built a kind of totem pole, complete with horoscope hieroglyphics, from thrown away beer and whiskey bottles. Another sculpture that still dazzled the eye on a bright clear afternoon was her towering, wheeling mobile of cast-off hubcaps found along county roads. Sometimes the wind caught them in the right angle to produce a strange falsetto voice that seemed to be calling lost souls. He had to admit there was something siren-like about Lou Ann. She had a big heart and liked to take in strays. Jelly just didn't want to be the stray de jour.

"I got things to do in town," he said and leaned forward into the window. "Thanks for the invite."

Lou Ann hunched forward and threw her arms over the wheel.

Jelly had seen that movement before in suspects he'd pulled over. Please, sit back, ma'am, he would have normally said but this was his sister and he was not really on duty. His smile stayed burning and she grinned back at him but his eyes changed focus through the gap in her wrap around of jean jacket and arms. There was a half-finished joint in the ashtray. He blinked and stepped away, not wanting to see more.

"I'll come by in a few days," he said.

"You do that, hon, just be sure and give me a call so I can clean the place up…plus, I guess I might as well tell you…"

Jelly waited and wiped the rain from his forehead.

"My friend Jack Turner…the sculptor, you remember him?"

"Sure…the biker guy."

"Yeah, he's coming down from Atlanta for a few months. He'll be staying with me while we work on some projects."

"Hey, that's good for you and him," Jelly said. "You two make a pretty good odd couple."

"Hey, don't push that analogy too far, little bro," she said and smiled with that look of finality. "Take care and say hi to Connie for me."

"You bet," Jelly said and stepped back as Lou Ann pulled away and scattered loose gravel in the circular drive. He watched her disappear down the county-maintained dirt road. By now she was probably sparking that number up and laughing to beat hell…thinking she got away with breaking the law. Well, she had…

Lou Ann sucked on the roach and blew smoke out the half open window. God love'm…he was always a cute baby and she sure thought he was fun to dress up and play with…until he started growing. And that name, Jelly, that was her invention 'cause she couldn't quite get that double-"l" going right. Jerry came out Jellie or later for writing, just as normal as could be, a nickname that stuck, Jelly. Funny that hang up on double r's. That must've been a past life as a Japanese concubine. Where else did all her sexual interests in Kama Sutra come from and all the things women could do to please each other without the ugly necessity of hairy warriors stripped of their armor. Those samurai beasts smelled of sweat and blood and bamboo and horses. Now there's a men's cologne for the ages, "Samurai"…make a bucket of that and sell it out of their shop in Atlanta, maybe out at Hartsfield Airport where folks need gifts for their loved ones.

Lou Ann brushed back her hair and swatted at a cinder floating off the roach. Things in her field of vision had taken on a lush warm color despite the gray rain. Jack was coming and that meant sacrifices as to space and tolerance for his demanding ways, his lists and all those got to get done rules for the day…Breakfast was like a briefing for the president. At least you got more shit done…but at the end of the day, like all those pundits on TV say, what do you gain? More trouble than a sack full of monkeys. More done, more to do.

Jelly was looking tired in the eyes. He was a sweet boy. But he was a cop through and through and what was all this lawyer shit. Probably trying to follow in the Russell side of the family and be like all them judges that presided over the courts in Warden for generations. Nasty bunch of tobacco spitting lawyers and their cronies in those old offices deep in the bottom of the courthouse. Reminded her of the catacombs in Rome. And that was just wrong. No place to go, no place to live…No wonder Jelly was looking anemic. He outta marry Connie and have a couple of kids. He was thirty something now…she tried to calculate but couldn't because she had to negotiate a left turn onto the highway and that took all her concentration. Thing was it was time to be cool about things and she kept her speed five miles under the limit and sat straight. She reached over and patted her purse. Down inside was her stash so recently refreshed by a happy visit with her oldest brother who was certainly putting his money where his mouth was. They were all turning outlaws just to survive. Bill…quoting Henry David Thoreau about civil disobedience. Wait 'til Jelly found out about this new skeleton in the closet. But Lou Ann Lovejoy would not be the messenger, no way, no how, no ma'am.

Jelly looked up at Bill's house. The image of his hulking, slumping brother headed down that dark hallway, that bothered him some. He knew at the back of that tunnel was his farm office, a mass of unfiled papers and bills and old farm equipment manuals…a manual typewriter for doing official business and boxes of shotgun shells and fishing gear and a long ago photo of him with Grandpa Sam after a Florida fishing trip, a huge string of red snapper tall as his thirteen year old frame. That long ago smile was nothing but an ancient memory now. Hopes of being one of the landed elite long gone. Now it was hand to mouth and a desperate funk hung around this place…with Bill's long days of pacing the acres, sitting in the woods and ignoring what he had to do…watching the inevitable converge into his present. There was no future greatness or salvation in the land for a farmer his size. But the stubborn bastard wouldn't let go of the hopeless dream. Jelly started back to the house to give their talk another go but his cell phone rang.

"Hey, redneck, what you doing?"

It was his partner Al Morris, his black buddy fellow detective.

"I'm getting out of the rain," Jelly said and slid into his cruiser. "The captain gave me the day off…well, on-call. Says I need a vacation."

"I been telling you that for a year, bud. You look like the ghost of Christmas past."

"So how's the vacation?"

"Oh man, me and the old lady and the kids hiked down to the bottom of the Grand Canyon. Oh my god, Jelly, talk about a hole in the ground…"

"It's gorgeous from all the pictures I've seen?"

"Oh yeah, it's just like the postcards but let me tell you, we just about croaked hiking back up to the rim…eleven miles on the Bright Angel Trail. Lord, the next day, we all lay in bed like cripples, like we had the polio."

Jelly laughed, seeing Al and wife Suzie and two young boys, writhing around in the motel. "So everything's going good…and how about that other thing?"

There was a pause and Al lowered his voice. "Yeah, I interviewed with the Flagstaff police. I gotta say it's really different out here for a black man. I was really impressed. Different atmosphere."

"You say yes?"

"Not yet. Told 'em I'd have to think it through and talk with Suzie. Pays good, benefits and the dry air might be good for the boys' asthma. I been thinking there's just too much pollution around Strickland what with all the poultry farms and crop dusting."

Jelly started his car and watched the wipers swipe clean the windows. He felt a heaviness settling in here in Bill's front yard. He needed to move on and get some fresh air through the partially lowered window. He began to ease down the drive and followed Lou Ann's tracks toward town.

"Well, makes sense then," Jelly agreed. "You gotta do right by your family."

"That's right but I don't like making decisions while still on vacation," Al said, his voice brightening. "I need to get back home and think things through. We all do."

"Well, you got the big green light from me," Jelly said and meant it. "You deserve the best, Al."

"You made up your mind about law school?"

"No…I'm really hung up here. I'm hoping a few days off will make things clearer."

"It sure helps to get away from down there," Al said. "Suzie's just glowing with enthusiasm…We haven't had so much fun since our honeymoon."

"That's great, Al."

The static began to eat into their talk. Jelly shook his phone and eased to a stop at the county four way. "Hey, you guys have a helluva time out there."

"We will...more fun than a barrel of monkeys," Al seemed to be shouting down a distant coiled trumpet. "Going to Vegas and then the flight home..."

"Hold on to your wallet, big guy," Jelly said, knowing Al's fascination with casino odds and how petty criminals subvert the games of chance.

"Got that old bad feeling, Jelly," Al said.

"About what?"

"About the hard asses round that county, you know what I mean?"

"Hey, you stick to Arizona and let me keep Georgia to a mild uproar. Relax...look who needs a vacation, eh?"

"All right, my man, you sounding good...but remember to keep those eyes open in the back of that empty head of yours."

"I'll see you next week, Al. Best to Suzie and the boys."

There was more static and then Al's voice was swallowed up by an electronic tumbleweed that swept him away. Everybody was warning him to watch his back. Maybe there was something to it.

Jelly tossed down the cell phone and studied the four-way stop. Every cardinal direction available and he wasn't sure where to go. What was it Yogi Berra said, when you come to a crossroads...just clear your mind and take it...

CHAPTER 9

▼

Bill Lovejoy squinted slightly through his powerful binoculars and watched his brother Jelly take the paved county road north. Good riddance, something fishy about him having the goddamned day off and this day, this Friday. Snooping around...like a bloodhound. The kid had been the center of attention of the family from the day he was born. My god, you'd think he was the Christ Arisen, the way Mama used to carry on about him. Ella and Lou Ann letting him sound off on everything, mister arbiter of the table conversation and the king of the TV remote. Little piss ant...No wonder he grew up to be a cop and now thinking of becoming a bloodsucking low life lawyer. Just another courthouse stool pigeon for the cops and the hard ass judges. Trying to reform people with punishment. Like we didn't have enough laws and poor assholes in jail. The last of the goddamned boom businesses in this leached out country was incarceration...prison building and support services. He'd had a chance to be a prison guard, no what do they call it, corrections officer. Corrections, my ass. Your ass, his ass, everybody's ass. That's what it came down to. Sodomy and murder. Now that's gonna set your values straight. This country was gone. Done. Finished. The New Americans were from everywhere else. Americans were becoming Chinese...except the Chinese owned the American debt. It was too late for most people, but if you had the cajones to do something about it...well, it didn't have to be that way. Innovation...the cutting edge...all those bullshit MBA terms coming out of TV commercials from Wall Street and the White House. You soulless bunch of assholes. Traitors to this country. Sucking at the tit of global corporations without any loyalties to Americans.

Bill walked across his crowded office and focused his binoculars on the far-away line of trees bisecting his frontage fields from the hundred acres running back to Sandy Creek. He moved slowly from left to right and right to left. No sign of any work back there. Yeah, he'd had to plow all the rows in reverse to get the maximum length and then to get the strip laid down to look the same as the other furrows while still compacting the earth. From the air with strewn hay it should look good for winter cover. And if these Mexican bird brains knew what they were doing…then they could bring the plane down tight over the trees and land without difficulty. Thank god he'd kept those old tobacco curing barns Daddy had built forty years ago. Civil disobedience…whatever it takes, Bill reflected on how he laid it out to Lou Ann…getting her oohs and aahs looking at the sheaves of plants drying from the rafters. Collective cells of dedicated revolutionaries…that's what American lived on. Revolution and it was time to spark up another civil war.

Bill rolled open his office window and lit up a large joint he pulled from his shirt pocket. He glanced at his office clock, a John Deere tractor centerpiece with large second sweep hand. Plenty of time before the wife came back from town with the kids and her work at Sammy's and driving that ugly goddamned yellow school bus. That was a fuckin' embarrassment to him to have that parked in their farmyard lot overnight. That meant poverty. And that, by all that was holy, was gonna goddamned be changed. Bill pulled on the joint and held the smoke in his lungs. Sweat popped out on his forehead. He felt his world swaying and flapping like a tattered flag in the wind.

Jelly considered the way west and north, roads out of the county and away from Warden. This was the way back to school, a way out of his family's miasma of relations, of all the dark things he had observed as a young cop on the beat, the darker motives of so-called good folk when push came to shove as a detective. Domestic violence calls were the worst. Even rougher than the drug busts. At least you knew going in with drug users that they were crazy and would do anything. With domestic disputes, the rage was so intense, so unpredictable, your nerves were strung tight waiting for the shotgun or pistol or knife. Nearer the deep nerve of attachment, of family and love and hate, and these motives overwhelmed common sense. A cop meant nothing to a man gone crazy over his woman's fidelity to him. The bonds were primitive and dark and bloody. Death was often the preferred solution.

Jelly cruised north for a bit through groves of pecans down Waters Road and when he hit the East West two-lane, he turned east toward Warden. Along here was the memory of an accident where he'd pulled two teens out of a car wrapped around a pine tree. They were still alive but died on the way to the hospital. Not far from that invisible marker on the road, he remembered a semi that hit a bridge abutment on Squally Creek, a dark iodine stained water, full of gar and brim. You'd often see blacks fishing in these rivers. It wasn't just a pastime, he'd long understood, the fish were a real supplement to their protein diet. Catfish were big mothers along here. That driver of the semi had fallen asleep and hit the abutment and nearly killed a family of black folk. They jumped into the creek and swam to safety but the driver burned to death, probably knocked unconscious and unable to get free. Burn victims, "crispy critters," that's what the hardened EMT guys called them. They were charred ash black and they usually had their hands extended to the steering wheel outward as if seeking some saving grace. God, what a way to go…

As he approached the city limit of Warden, Jelly looked outward toward the old white frame Baptist church of Mount Olive. Mostly white Baptists attended this historical church with its big graveyard behind. Most of the early settlers in the county and city were buried out here. So were the Lovejoys and Russells, both ancestral clans. Jelly pulled off the road onto the grassy shoulder and eased down the narrow dirt rutted road toward the church. Out in the back he saw a funeral tent and gravediggers at work on a new grave.

It was still morning and he wanted to have lunch with Connie. He parked the car and got out and walked around the church and put in a call on his cell. The sun was coming out now, the misty skies clearing.

"Hey you," Connie answered in her bright, upbeat voice. "Long time no hear…or see."

"Been working hard. You with a patient?"

"Kinda. I'm at the nurse's station. Just a minute." A door closed and the din of the hospital corridor faded.

"Listen, I'd like to buy you lunch. When do you get a break?"

"Twelve-thirty…the usual hour."

"You guys busy?"

"It's been nuts around here. Lots more drug problems."

"You seeing meth skeletons."

"Bathtub meth…hon, the worst of all."

"That's due to the fine work of our crystal meth wars."

"I'm telling you, we've got a major problem in this county."

"Okay, how 'bout the Pig 'n' Whistle for some barbeque. I'll pick you up outside emergency. Twelve thirty."

"Sounds good. I could use some protein and a down home atmosphere."

Jelly rang off and walked out through the graves and their narrow walled corridors. He stepped lively to avoid the swatches of sandspurs. Back to the right he found his family plots. He stood and looked over the generations of names going back to the mid 1800s when the first settlers mostly Scot-Irish came west from Savannah and Jacksonville. These were names etched on old eroded sandstone and slate markers. Great-great grandpa Tate was the grandfather to Jelly's Granny Rose. Grandpa Tate was a famous preacher in his time, known for his inspired sermons, a man without formal education but self-taught, a man "called" to preaching the gospel in the old sing-song, ecstatic tradition. Granny Rose often despaired that his style of a natural calling to preaching was gone now, replaced by the formal written notes of college educated, seminary preachers.

"Ain't got the spirit, the fire," she'd say.

Over a few yards was the grave of Jelly's cousin, Henry Parker. He stood there in some kind of mute prayer, seeing his poor cousin decomposing with his shattered skull. Jelly felt his chest tightening and he shook his head and walked away and tried to focus his eyes on the other markers but he made little sense of what he was seeing. He kept walking and when he looked up he was near the gravediggers.

"Hey officer," a young black man said, wiping sweat off his forehead. "You come for this boy's funeral?"

Jelly saw the young black kid looking at his blazer open, caught by the wind, revealing his hip pistol. "No, who is he?"

The others stopped working and watched him. There were two black men and two Mexicans.

"They gonna be burying that Jessie Alsop," the young black kid said. "That war hero."

"The one that won all them medals in the war on terror over there in the Near East," the older black man spoke up.

"That was last year he came back, wasn't it?" Jelly said.

"Yes sir, he came back with nary a serious scratch," the older man noted.

"I remember the ceremony on the courthouse square," Jelly said. "I must've missed the obits for this past week. What happened to him?"

The young black man spat into a mound of yellow red clay. "I hear he took an overdose of some drugs. When they found him he'd been dead for a day or two out in the county."

Jelly felt like he'd already been on vacation and missed an entire chapter in the town's gossip.

"Well, that's a real shame," Jelly said. "He must be in his early twenties."

The older black man said, "Yeah, looking at the gravestone…looks like he was going on twenty-three. That's way too young, I reckon."

"For sure," Jelly said and squinted at the older man. He couldn't remember his name right away but in his first year as a patrolman he'd busted him in a break-in. He'd gone away for a three year stint, being a repeat offender. Boggs…wasn't it…he couldn't get the name just right. Yeah, Amos Boggs. "Sometimes it's more dangerous in your own backyard I guess…"

"That's for sure," the young guy said and the older man nodded in agreement. "He was good at dodging bullets way over there but when it come to the drugs…they must've been too much for him."

"Service this afternoon?"

"Two o'clock. Looks like the sun's gonna come out for Jessie's folks."

They all stood there as if in silent prayer over the empty grave.

"Well, you fellahs have a good day," Jelly said.

"You too, Officer," Amos Boggs said and eyed him straight on, letting him know he remembered too.

Jelly winked and moved off. Connie would know something about this case. He got back to his car and slumped into the front seat. What the hell was happening to his memory? Where had he been when all this was coming down? Asleep at the wheel?

He sat for a minute listening to the wind through the needles of the tall slash pines, "like nature's violins" his Mama used to say, and he closed his eyes and tried to remember the last time he wasn't eaten up by chronic discontent. Taking time off took practice and he knew he had a lot to learn.

Amos Boggs watched the white cop slump in his car out front of the church. Something in him wanted to sight his hunting rifle on that pretty white head and explode it like a rotten Halloween pumpkin. Not that this white punk now a detective deserved it more than the rest. But that fire of ten years before was gone. No sir, the murder of a white cop was certain death long before getting to the midnight of the electric chair or whatever they was doing to kill people now. Was it injection? It was always the next thing. Maybe a swift lynching was a better death than these strung out appeals cases where you sat on death row and couldn't smoke a cigarette 'cause it was bad for your fuckin' health! What a sick goddamned joke.

What was that Jerry Lovejoy…yeah, that was his name…used to be a big shot halfback in high school football. He remembered the cold night when the high school won the state semi-finals and this Lovejoy or one of them…made the final touch down. Integrated sports. Never thought I'd see the day. For a minute there it all seemed like things were gonna work out for people down here. But that was high school. Out on the street, no job to speak of, never enough money…what the fuck did they expect them to do? Wait 'til God threw down manna from Heaven?

One smooth click of the trigger and that boy would be history and there'd be a new opening in the police department. And fat chance a black brother with a record was gonna get squat from that job opportunity. Shit. More likely one of these wetbacks here will get the job. Amos eyed the two Mexicans just added to the payroll by Haycroft Funeral Home. Bet they didn't damn well have working papers. Could barely speak a word of English.

"Quien es?" the older of the two Mexicans said and nodded toward Lovejoy in his car now starting to move.

"Cop," Amos Boggs said and spat into the grave. "Shot his cousin dead at twelve years old."

The Mexican nodded with black, cold-eyed understanding and translated for the other man. "Sí, la policía." He and his buddy spat into the grave in unison.

"Murderer," said the older black man with finality.

"Asesino," came the translation.

CHAPTER 10

▼

Back in Warden, ensconced in a dark tall wooden booth at the Pig 'n' Whistle, Jelly smiled at Connie. Country music blared in full force over the PA system and the hubbub of a full crowd of hungry carnivores inflated the noise to a low roar. Conversations were definitely confidential.

"It's good to see you again," Jelly said. "I guess you think I'd gone into hibernation."

Connie held the greasy plastic menu gingerly between two fingers.

"You know how many bacteria are on the average menu?"

"Most of the town's germs, I imagine. Good for the immune system, right?"

"Oh, you're so smart. I knew you were off in your law books prepping for those law school interviews."

"I was for a while and then I just fell off the cliff and haven't really recovered. I don't know what I'm going to do."

"Don't you have to make a decision soon?"

The waitress, Edna Brooks, a widow of thirty-five, slouched up to their table with her protruding pot belly.

"Well if ain't Colombo and his private duty nurse."

Jelly and Connie laughed. Edna was a character and as such was allowed an embarrassing degree of leeway. Her husband had been a minor NASCAR driver but was killed in a pit accident. A tire flew off another car at a hundred miles an hour and crushed her husband Bobby's head. Everyone tried to humor her morbid view of life now. Bitterness was her daily liquor.

"Edna, my dear, how are you?" Jelly asked.

"Like warmed over death, that's how I feel."

She smirked in great imitation of a recent president of the US and held aloft her BIC pen over her order pad.

"Sorry to hear that," Jelly said. "Hope it isn't contagious."

"I wouldn't tell you about it if I knew," Edna returned and brushed back her black hair streaked with purple tints.

Connie said, "I'll have the Buffalo Burger and fries and a medium diet Coke."

"Like you need to diet," Edna said and craned her neck to get a better view of Connie's Rubenesque, curvy body in her tight nurse's uniform. Edna's middle was filling out and her slouch had taken on a new degree of depression. A lariat around her neck held a whistle. When the owner, Odell Sikes, felt in a generous mood, he'd have Edna hit the whistle good and loud and announce a free meal to a diner based on a random draw of tickets. Of course everyone suspected Bob took a quick look at the size of the Bar B Q order before making his, ahem, random draw.

"I'll have the Memphis ribs and extra cole slaw, regular Coke, large," Jelly said, already tasting the delicious sweet meat peeling away from the bone. "Oh and don't hold back on the hot sauce."

"Right, gotcha, you never change," Edna said.

"You don't either, hon," Jelly said and winked.

"Some of your buddies are in the back over there, lawman."

"Oh yeah," Jelly said and leaned out of the booth and took a quick look. It was the Chief of Police and a couple of his assistants and an agent from the Georgia Bureau of Investigation.

"Those are big shots," Jelly said. "They don't care about a nobody rookie detective."

"Wonder why I hear your name coming up every time I pass by," Edna said and lowered her face to give him a knowing look from her dark brown eyes.

"Maybe they're thinking of giving him a promotion," Connie said with pride. "He's the best they got."

"Or maybe he's in a pit of quicksand and the nastiness is sucking him down," Edna said and laughed at Connie's darkened face. "Gotcha there, Connie."

"Get out of here, Edna," Connie said and shook her head. "You're worse than a hill of fire ants."

Edna's manic smile broke out. "Ain't I, though!"

Edna left them and drifted among the tables toward the kitchen in the back. Jelly tried to get Edna's gossip out of his mind. What indeed was the Chief talking about with the GBI…the state equivalent of the FBI? He drew an uneasy blank and heard Connie's talk as at a distance.

"So what's the decision on law school?" Connie said, getting his full attention, reopening the old scab wound of career ambition.

"I've been a detective now for one year and I don't think it's time to jump into something else. Although, I'm thirty and setting up a law career gets harder with every year. I'm already behind our generation. You know that."

"That's partly just attitude," Connie said. "But you have a point."

"And I don't won't to leave town and give up what we've had all these years."

All these years meant being boyfriend and girlfriend, off and on, since junior high school. That's when they first danced and first kissed and first petted beyond those acceptable public displays of affection. And then in their twenties they became more intimate but because of the pill, they'd been able to maintain a sexual intimacy, through hot and cold romantic periods of war and détente. Now they were in a cooling off period.

Connie stared at him, resting her chin in her propped up hands. Her blue eyes, normally an ice blue, now looked like a washed out sky. She was his age but already he could see wrinkles around the eyes, deeper lines in her once baby face. The years of nursing, odd shifts and the stress of trauma care, all that effort to nurture the local population and help her retired mother and father financially. Not to say she lacked charm and sexual allure. No. She still had that hour-glass voluptuousness in her small body frame. She was tough. And he admired her stamina for the long haul and sharp intelligence under pressure.

"I'm reluctant to leave because of Mom and Dad," she said slowly. "We've been over this. But that doesn't mean I can't be supportive."

"Supportive?"

"You know what I mean. Supportive in career, supportive emotionally too."

"You mean in love?"

"Do you mean in love with me?"

Jelly swallowed and Edna arrived with the food.

"Don't let me interrupt the love birds," she said. "Just remember, you can't trust men, Connie. They're all lying dogs."

"Thanks, Edna," Connie said. "I'll try and keep that in mind."

"Enjoy, kids," she said and vanished into the blooming buzzing noon customers.

"Are you really in love with me, Jelly?" she said and tilted her head and smiled at him in her prim, knowing way.

"Yes, I love you, Connie," he said. "I've always loved you more than any other girl…woman, that is."

She laughed. "Well, thanks for the promotion to womanhood. Remember I'm your age too. We're not getting younger and this is when the nesting instinct kicks in big time...especially for a woman. The bio clock is ticking for kids and family life."

"I hear you. I guess my career thing is just the male aspect of that."

"I suppose. I just wonder if you're using this career thing as a way of postponing your commitment to the rest of life. I mean some men don't really want the responsibility of a wife and children."

"How's that?"

"I mean, maybe you had enough of family growing up as a Lovejoy."

"What's wrong with us Lovejoys?"

"I'm not answering that one. I think you know the answers to that. You being the baby of the family and all..."

Jelly colored in embarrassment. "Okay, I'm avoiding the big questions. I admit I need to make a decision but I just feel like floating between the career choices will resolve itself into an obvious answer."

Connie took a bite of her burger and chewed thoughtfully while Jelly began to eat.

"Why not a hybrid choice, rather that either or?"

"You mean part time marriage, part time work?"

"No!" Connie blurted, unheard beyond their booth. "I mean part-time police work, part-time law school. Can't you find a law school nearby where you can take courses on say a halftime basis?"

"Yeah, but that takes forever. I'd never have any free time."

"Well, let's talk about something else..."

Jelly felt relieved. "I want to talk with you more...but not here. How about later tonight. You good for a stay over at my place tonight?"

Connie frowned in doubt. "My parents expect me home tonight..."

"But you're thirty and they can't tell you what to do."

"No, they can't. I'll have to think it over and see."

"That's fair enough."

"So what are you up to today wandering around on call?"

"It's been a weird day so far...say, I was out at Mount Olive Church and they were getting ready to bury Jessie Alsop, that National Guard soldier back from the Near East. You know anything about his death?"

Connie bit her lower lip in thought. "It was an overdose of crystal meth. Burst his heart and lungs. The family wanted it hushed up. He was apparently under treatment for post traumatic stress. His mother told one of the trauma nurses that he felt sick about killing civilians over there, women and kids. He didn't know what he was doing and they panicked under fire. He just couldn't get over the deaths. That's what she said but there were..." and her Connie leaned forward, "signs of bruising similar to what you might find with someone trying to escape from being tied up."

"How did I miss this whole thing?" Jelly said.

"The family asked the army to keep it quiet and they came in to take care of the explanations. I imagine the Chief just went along with the military. What's your partner Al Morris think?"

"He's on vacation out west with his family in Arizona. That's the cover story for an interview with Flagstaff police. I think he likes it out there."

"I can imagine," Connie said, leaning forward to whisper. "Probably less career discrimination. He's got a wife and kids to think about."

Jelly took Connie's hand and kissed it.

"Why, thank you, gallant sir."

"Come and see me tonight, won't you?"

"You're mighty persuasive, detective, but I'm just a young innocent Southern gal with little knowledge of the real world."

"Uh huh, Nurse Sorensen, then it's time to teach this village idiot what little you know about the carnal world."

"Goodness, you do go on. But I do love a man with a pistol and a gold shield."

"Dazzling tools bewitching to Southern Belles?"

"Just something sexy about a man of the law at high noon..."

"Or midnight?"

"Do tell, suh."

Outside the Pig 'n' Whistle Connie sat in Jelly's car and watched as Jelly spoke with the Chief of police. The chief and his entourage had exited just after them. Now the Chief was glancing her way with a polite nod and toothy smile.

Edna had blown her Pig 'n' Whistle and surprise, the free meal had gone to the Chief's table. He was sucking on a toothpick and giving her the once over. Creepy old man. Knew too much about people and all their bad habits. There came a time when old men like that needed to retire. Jelly was listening and nodding.

Jelly got in the car and started it.

"What's that old fart want with you?" Connie said.

Jelly laughed. "Guess he's not on your hit parade."

"He gives me the creeps."

"He wants me to do a community outreach thing with Officer Gomez later this afternoon. A meeting with the new Mexican priest over at St. Matthew's."

"Isn't Gomez a woman cop?"

"Yeah, so what? She speaks Spanish and she's on the patrol force for their barrios."

"Why you?"

Jelly drove around the Pig 'n' Whistle drive-in circle and pulled into traffic toward the hospital.

"Why me? He wanted a detective and a patrol officer to meet with the padre…and he remembered I'd picked up some Spanish."

"She's kinda pretty, isn't she?"

"I hadn't noticed," Jelly said and kept his eyes straight ahead.

"I believe I've met her in the emergency room a couple of times," Connie said. "She's got quite a figure. Is she single?"

Jelly laughed. "Hey, what is this?"

Connie smiled. "I'm just being jealous."

"I like that."

"She's not your type anyway."

"Oh and how do you know that, mi señorita?"

"She's probably a lesbian."

"Oh mama!"

"A little S&M with handcuffs."

"Hey, you're getting me hot now."

She punched him in the arm as they pulled up to the emergency entrance.

"Oh my god, well, back to work," Connie said and kissed Jelly on the lips quickly.

"Call me on my cell when you want me to pick you up."

"Don't rush the schedule, Officer…You be careful now."

"You too."

She left him and saw him pull away. She went to the bathroom and washed up. She'd pull the afternoon coverage in E.R. probably, depending on what was needed.

When she came out of the bathroom, she heard shouts and screams. She ran down the hall. Inside ER was bedlam. She heard a male voice moaning in a horrific cry.

"Godammit! Help me!!!"

She rushed into the triage room and found two burn victims being wrapped into rubber gelatin sheets. A doctor was injecting morphine into two men.

Nurses were trying to restrain the badly burned men, their charred clothes stuck to their brilliant red ghastly flesh.

"What happened?" Connie whispered to the head nurse.

She turned a hard eye on Connie.

"Fuckin' meth lab blew up…stupid bastards…"

The smell of burning human flesh never left your memory or was any easier to take. Experience didn't lessen the horror. Connie swallowed her gag reflex and focused on assisting the team, moving the victims down the hall to critical care. When she staggered out of the room a few minutes later she found herself staring at the Chief of Police in the admitting area surrounded by his aides and the Georgia Bureau of Investigation detective. He was a heavy set man with a bulldog face. He wasn't listening to the Chief but staring right at her with his cold, button black eyes. Suddenly she felt a chill run through her body and her fear wasn't for herself but for Jelly.

CHAPTER 11

▼

Sammy's was a well-known bookstore in Warden. Before Jelly's older brother Sammy had bought it, then known as Books & News, it had been the only bookstore in the town. Now as Jelly parked his car in the angled spot outside his brother's store, he remembered the old place as it had been years before...with its poker room upstairs in the back. Down the side street East off the courthouse square, across from it within living memory was the last livery stable where a farmer could buy a good plowing mule. As a kid Sammy liked to talk about the wonderful smell of fresh manure of an early morning. Sammy was thirty six now, six years older than Jelly, four years younger than Ella who was now forty. One of the games Jelly played was calculating everyone's birthday with the change of the seasons. After all, he was bringing up the rear...and that somehow seemed important to him. In fact, as the youngest, he had to admit he was somewhat egocentric in thinking his four siblings formed a kind of spiral around him and his movements through life...as if they were mutually monitoring each other's progress to the grave.

Jelly stepped through the double doors behind the tinted front windows and breathed in the smell of newsprint, books and tobacco and sundries. It was a kind of incense that he associated with his older, more scholarly brother who liked good cigars and pipes. He was the reader and family historian and family philosopher...but all self-taught. He'd not stayed in college long. He didn't like being tested and left the university for life in Warden...first at the newspaper and then here at Books & News. He married a girl from Tallahassee he'd met in college but she didn't like being away from her Momma and Daddy and their car dealership money...and left him. He'd never remarried, had girlfriends but didn't make the marriage effort again. If his heart was broken, he kept it to himself, living in the little house in Warden where he'd started out. When old man Stark died, Sammy had managed to buy the place and promptly changed the name and upgraded with a wider selection of good books, more gift ideas and candy and tobacco. He'd put in a reading section for children in the front corner where mothers could keep an eye on their kids and he'd piped in soft classical music and easy listening. He even hung air freshening machines around the big long room with its tin flowered patterned ceiling to keep the air sharp and "minds clear." His business had prospered and he'd hired family members to help out.

"Our wandering guardian angel," Sammy called out from behind his elevated desk and office. "What brings you here on a busy Friday?"

"I'm on-call today," Jelly said. "Thought I'd drop in and get my dose of the gossip from the merchant streets."

Sammy had longish hair, slightly graying, and pushed up his glasses along his nose with his thumb. He blinked behind his smudged lenses.

"Look who's here," Jelly heard behind him and turned to embrace his sister-in-law Celia, Bill's wife, who worked her part-time afternoons before the final bus run of the school afternoon. Celia smelled of fresh ink and paper. She was slim and pale and her blonde brown hair was tied up in a bun; not a bad looking woman, she carried her worries in her face with long deep lines in her cheeks. She was unpacking paperbacks books from boxes on the floor, placing them in turn racks. "I talked to Bill earlier. He said you and Lou Ann come by…"

Jelly smiled. No secrets for long in this family. "Had to hear my big bro's rant and rave for the month."

Sammy tapped his forehead with a pencil. "Let me guess, Federal obstruction of States rights, the downward spiral of the small farmer, the death of the pioneer spirit?"

Celia said, "You sound like you wrote his speeches."

Sammy smiled, his buck teeth protruding. "I did but I ain't never been paid."

Celia shook her finger at Sammy. "Now you know Bill's got a thing about paying his debts."

"Tell me about it," Sammy said. "And he was darn good at collecting his debts too."

"Take it out of your hide," Jelly said.

"Hell, he was worse than Daddy," Sammy said. "And that's saying something about the puritan nature of this family of ingrates."

"Hey, watch that," Jelly said. "Mostly Bill was on his soap box about legalizing marijuana cultivation."

"Now that's a new twist for the great agrarian," Sammy said.

Celia was frowning. "I wish you wouldn't repeat that, Jelly. I told him to shut up about that idea. Nothing but trouble. And you a lawman...can you imagine how dumb he is to talk like that."

A pause ensued as Sammy and Jelly made eye contact. Sammy slowly smiled. "Don't you worry, Celia, he's crazy but he ain't that far gone...yet."

"Well, you know how the gossip runs around this town," Celia said and wiped her hands on her work apron. "Not a secret kept in this sorry old place of Warden."

"Well, don't you worry," Sammy said. "Blood's thicker than water. He's our own nasty oldest brother."

Celia shrugged and faded down an aisle to help a customer who'd come inside, the front door bell tinkling.

"So what's happening?" Jelly said.

"Hell, you outta know more than me," Sammy said. "What's the word from the street?"

"Ax Man's coming back," Jelly said. "Gonna bring a whole lotta trouble with him."

Sammy's eyes bugged out. "Now how about that. Guess what's playing over at the old Starlight?"

"No idea."

"Creature from the Black Lagoon."

"No kidding...our old favorite."

"Yeah, they've got a horror classic series running all this weekend. You wanna go?"

"When's the Creature showing?"

"There's a matinee at three-thirty. Only a ninety minute film, if that. I can check. I've got the film history book over here. Thought I'd take Celia's kids to see it. They love movies."

"Okay, I got an errand I gotta run not long after that. A thing for the Chief...but I may show up."

"No big deal, sleuth..."

"I'm just nosing around like a bloodhound today."

"Looking for the scent of evil?"

"Maybe...not sure."

"Don't worry, there's plenty of mischief going on around this old town."

"Nothing you'd want to share."

Sammy shrugged. "Nobody talks to me. They figure I've gotta be bug nuts to try to compete with the Barnes & Noble and Waldenbooks at the Mall. I'm a relic…but then they don't sell tobacco and lottery tickets."

"Speaking of tobacco," Jelly said, teasing with a smile. "You wouldn't happen to have any Cubans on hand?"

"I wish," Sammy said. "But I've got something for you to try…these natural tobacco Indian cigars. Great flavor…a little sweet…They're not too pretty but I think you might enjoy them. No additives. Put out by an Indian reservation up in North Carolina. Cherokees, I think."

Sammy handed Jelly a foil pack.

"What do I owe you?"

"Gimme a break."

"Can't accept gifts, against the police ethics code."

"Arrest me then," Sammy said.

"Another time when I'm not on-call," Jelly said. "By the way, the Chief forced me to take a couple weeks of vacation beginning Monday."

"Damn…paid vacation. What's that feel like?"

"I'm not sure I know," Jelly said. "But I'll give you a detailed report."

"Hey, take Connie and get out of this place. Go down to Key West or the Bahamas."

"I don't have that kind of money saved."

"Nobody does. You wait 'til you're flush, you'll be too tired and old to go."

He gave his brother a sideways hug. "Thanks for the smokes. If I don't see you later, have a good weekend, okay?"

"Don't forget about the Ax Man's buddy, the Creature from the Black Lagoon."

"Oh yeah," Jelly said, blushing at his forgetfulness. "I'll do my best to get there."

"See you later, hon," Celia called.

Jelly blew her a kiss. "Take care."

"Where you headed now?" Sammy said. "No, let me guess, the courthouse and Friday afternoon criminal case review."

"You're a master mind reader."

"You'd be one too if you lived your life near the courthouse day in and day out. I'm a tethered myopic circus bear…"

"And the town loves your exhibit. You're a town fixture now."

"I was afraid of that," Sammy said and walked his brother to the door. "Weather's clearing for the time being."

"More hurricane remnants coming up from the Gulf though."

"Life's a beach…" Sammy said. "And say, try one of those cigars…just don't inhale."

"That's been questionable legal advice in the past."

"Not for good ol' boys."

Sammy rang up the local bestseller, "Crusade for Freedom," an account of a Medal of Honor Marine who fought in Iraq. A teen girl was buying it for her grandfather who was a veteran, "for his birthday, he was in Viet Nam." Sammy nodded.

"That's mighty nice, you come back, now."

"Oh, I will. I love to read," she said.

God love you then…Sammy prayed and closed the cash register. If anything were clear, this was a civilization headed back to oral culture, especially for the working and lower middle classes. Who had time to finish a book anymore? Well, maybe an old bachelor like himself. Hey, you were married once…he cajoled himself…could happen again. Hope to hell not, another critic said.

But this Marine author…Jason Hollister, II, he was selling well. A member of Hollister's Marine's unit was going to speak at the Rotary Dinner at the Strickland Hotel that evening. Sammy, one of the few libertarians around, had his issues with the crusade nonsense. He'd read enough about Christian history in the Middle Ages to suffer no illusions about reforming the cultures of the Bible. But he hated not getting together with his courthouse square business cronies and sharing a meal and the local concerns…lower taxes and easier parking for clients. Keeping your face in their faces kept you protected from surprises and unhappy gossip. Lately he'd been getting plenty of sympathy from the independent business people with all the strip mall franchise pressure.

Celia stepped behind the counter and leaned on the desk.

"You okay?" he asked her.

"I'm just feeling weird. Don't know what it is, Sammy."

"You want off early, go ahead. I can handle things."

"No…hon, I'd just as soon be here in the bookstore as out at the house with Bill's wintertime funk."

"SAD. Seasonal affective disorder, Celia. I've said that before. My brother is like our great uncle Dennis. He was a bastard come the fall and winter. Blew his brains out one day down back of the barn."

Celia blanched and hung her head.

"I'm sorry," Sammy said. "I got the sensitivity of a concrete block. I don't think Bill would ever go that far. He just gets angry and then broods while getting even with all his enemies."

"That's what I'm afraid of…I just can't take the torture he's been in."

"He outta be on tranquilizers, anti-depressants. Hell, there's millions of people suffer winter depression. Truth is, Bill never has been the comedian of the family."

"Who was?" Celia said. "You?"

"Me? Naw, I'm too stuffy and pedantic, always minding everybody's business…I'd say the comic of the family is sitting right out there."

Sammy pointed through the bookstore window across the street and traffic; on the corner Jelly sat on a park bench on the courthouse square practically in the shadow of the old confederate statue.

"Jelly?"

"Believe it or not. He used to be a kick and a half. That all changed after his hunting incident."

"Oh yeah, that was such a shame. Poor Henry. Poor Jelly. It was an accident."

"Doesn't matter. Completely knocked that sense of humor and goofiness out of him. Look at him now. He's up there dreaming about all the family ghosts that ever trod across those dusty footpaths in the shadow of the courthouse. You don't even want to know the details. He's really our family historian."

Celia smiled. "Now there's bound to be an argument there. I always see you with the genealogy charts and all those notes for your book on the Lovejoy history."

"There's a difference. I'm just a collector of facts and papers. I don't really have a vivid imagination of all these people. That's why it doesn't bother me to read all these books in here…" His hand swept the bookstore. "I need them to have an imagination. Think of all the work these writers have done for us."

"It is amazing. Sometimes I look at all these books and wonder why in the world things aren't better than they are."

"Jelly's the dreamer, the real historian in the clan. He sees the old folk and all their troubles and triumphs. Sometimes I wonder if he's gonna be okay. He's not happy with his life so far."

Celia said softly, "None of my business but I think he outta marry Connie and get his law degree."

"You're a better matchmaker than me."

"Your sister Ella's the best matchmaker I ever met."

Sammy smiled. "She's a caution, that woman. No telling where she got that gift but she does indeed have a knack for reading people. She could be an on-line psychic without a hitch, but she'd never consider something so crass. That reminds me, she's supposed to come into town this afternoon and bring Dahlia to see the doctor."

"God she loves that colored woman like a sister. They been together since they were teen girls."

"It's something you don't see as much these days. It was more common way back before integration. Kind of like a lady in waiting servant that becomes your lifelong shadow."

"Now there's something for your history book."

"They're probably planning to have dinner here in town. You wanna come along."

"No, hon, I'll do my bus run and then get dinner ready out at the farm for my grumpy gang."

Sammy felt a pang of loss looking at Celia. She would have made a good wife for himself; he'd have treated her better than Bill. Bill had a heart cold as grave-yard marble at his core.

"I sure appreciate your helping me out here afternoons," Sammy said.

"Well, thank you, hon, I really appreciate the opportunity. I never realized how much fun retail work was, especially what I thought was boring old books. I stand corrected on that."

"Take as many as you can read home…like I say, a good bookseller is a good reader. You'll sell more books here if you're personally enthusiastic."

He patted Celia on her wrinkled hands with their red knuckles.

"You've been real nice to me, Sammy."

"Hey, what are brother-in-laws for? We gotta stick together in these low times."

"Praise the Lord on that one," Celia said and brushed back a wisp of loose gray hair that had fallen across her lean cheek and almost seemed to leave a permanent shadow.

CHAPTER 12

▼

Jelly puffed on the sweet tasting cigar. Indian tobac. Not bad but it probably ate your teeth out after, oh, twenty years or so. Big deal. By then you didn't care if you had a youthful smile. You weren't young, you'd never be young again.

This spot near the confederate soldier was one of his favorites as it had been for unknown numbers of his male ancestors. Old codgers used to make a habit of sitting around the courthouse square and replaying their glory days. An old tradition but he was wondering what had happened to that ritual. Old folks stayed in their apartments or homes and watched TV. It was hard to get them out, even though the city of Warden provided a special bus service to bring them downtown to the senior center. The more the town tried to do in this old fashioned effort to bring the history back, the more pathetic the final deed. The center of the city was abandoned except for younger and middle-aged people shopping, and even that was dying off with the malls out on the bypass, and what was left were government offices, trust banks and attorneys and doctors and dentist offices.

Jelly aimed his cigar at the corner near the old magnolia that had been planted a century before. Just about there his great grandfather Lovejoy had had an argument with another oldster of his generation, two sons of civil war veterans, he guessed. And these eighty something retired farmers, back in the thirties, nothing to do but hang around the courthouse square and spit tobacco, they unearthed an old clan sore spot. A matter of a fence dispute between their fathers that had never been resolved and passed over by them in their heydays, too busy and reasonable to care…it being a matter of a mere few feet where this corner of a field came to a vertex and an exit from plowing to the county road. But now in their ancient wisdom his great grandfather Thomas had heard just about all he could take from Franklin Flag...and standing up they had come face to face in their rhetoric and without a second to waste, Thomas Lovejoy flashed a long handled razor from an ivory sheath and swiped the belly protruding from the white shirt of his opponent and to the stunned amazement and horror of the attending elders, Franklin Flags' blue gray guts spilled through his hands onto the dirt and spare grass of the tobacco-stained courthouse yard.

Jelly smoked the Indian cheroot and closed his eyes. There must have been quite a scene following that. Doctors certainly and of course the sheriff and his deputies must have been called in to clear the scene. Newspaper reports were sparse and cryptic. As Jelly remembered it, "The opponents to the land dispute resolved their disagreements in an equitable manner and all charges were dropped."

When Jelly opened his eyes, across from him on the opposite bench was old Mister Fuller, one of the half dozen centenarians of the town. A black man with a few tufts of wizened white wooly hair. One eye was closed permanently, the other was a blur of colors. He sat on the bench in his nearly sightless manner, bent forward on a rubber tipped cane, and chanted a ditty:

> Red headed woodpecker
>
> Sitting on a pine
>
> Wants a chaw tobacco
>
> But he can't have mine.

Old Fuller sniffed the air and said, "Now that smells mighty good."

Jelly offered him one and he accepted and Jelly lit it for him. Fuller breathed the aroma deep and exhaled.

"Can't hurt you at my age," he said and smiled. "I thank you."

"Indian tobacco. Supposed to be clean. Good for you."

"Uh huh," Mr. Fuller said and smiled and spit out a strand of loose tobacco from the curled stock. "It does seem home rolled. Kinda sweet too."

"How's your eyesight, Mister Fuller?"

"Oh, I don't see much anymore but I sure hear more than a plenty."

"You don't miss much, do you?"

"Oh I just walk around and eat groceries," he said with a slight smile. "Who have I the pleasure of speaking with, sir?"

"Jerry...Jelly...Lovejoy."

Old Man Fuller hung his head in thought and licked the tip of the cigar. "Well, I know the Lovejoys going way back to the twenties I imagine. Old Thomas Lovejoy and Sam and his brothers up toward Valdosta and Thomasville."

"That's the clan."

"And you're the grandson of old Sam Lovejoy?"

"Yes sir."

"I worked for both your daddy and his daddy. Field work, odds and ends. Heck, I worked for half the people in this old town. Used to haul bails of cotton 'cross town for fifty cents and lemme tell you that was good money in the Thirties."

"Who you living with now?"

"I got a grand niece lives over here in Sunset Village. She keeps a room for me. She's a good cook too. I just try to stay out of the way of the young people."

"Well, you're a walking history book for this Warden. I'll bet the town historical museum would love to have you talk about the old days."

"You know I was thinking the same thing and you know the old ladies over there one Christmas says, hey now, Mister Fuller, we have children in the audience so please now…don't be vulgar…Oh no ma'am, I'm just a good old nigger and all the piss and vinegar done gone from me. Wish I could have seen her pink white face but my diabetes was causing my sight to fail by then "

"What did you say to the kids?"

"Oh you know, stay in school, get as much education as you can 'cause nobody can take that away from you. You should've heard the applause. After that there was some talk of coffee and cake and all I could hear was running feet and chairs being folded fast and furious. I did get a good cup of coffee, gotta say."

Jelly laughed. "So, tell me, what's your impression of the Lovejoys as a clan?"

Fuller looked in Jelly's direction and focused his one good eye. "You a young man, I suppose."

"Thirty."

"Oh my, just a breeze 'cross the trees. What you do, son?"

"I'm a cop. A detective with the Strickland County police."

Fuller puffed on his cigar. "I do believe I heard things about you among my people. Good things. You're a fair man, they say."

"I'm glad to hear that."

"Well, that's how I'd rate the other Lovejoys. Hard workers all. Fair pay for a fair day's work. Mostly farmers the ones I knew. Didn't used to hear the Lovejoy name in the town too much, 'cept round farmer's market days. They was some cotton and tobacco brokers too. Used to see them playing checkers for quarters waiting for shipments. But what's the name on your Mama's side?"

"The Russells."

Mister Fuller sat up straight and leaned back on the bench.

"Now I know why I'm finding you up here at the county courthouse. Years back there was a passel of Russells what was lawyers and judges. Russells, they're out the west side of the county round about Harmony and Payne. Big landowners and you didn't want to be on their bad list, no sir."

"I'm not that familiar with them."

"Uh huh, there's lots nobody knows about folks with that much money and time on their hands."

"You remember the case of divorce here back in the Twenties and the big trouble here in the courthouse?"

"Lord I hadn't thought about that in so long. I was working down the livery stable and we heard the shots and everybody come running up here. There was blood everywhere in that courtroom. That was Russell trouble, son. Good you on the right side of the law. Trouble is, trouble keeps rollin' around this old town and you never know who's gonna be next. Me, I try to forget all that bad stuff and enjoy my days...the few I got left."

"You surprised you lived this long?" Jelly asked him.

"I'm can't believe it half the time. Ain't a lot of fun neither. Ain't hardly nobody that remembers how things was when we was boys and girls...but then, given the chance I wouldn't give it up. There's advantages to living a long life as long as you keep your mind and don't piss you pants. I got good ears. I was a musician in my youth and middle age. Used to play the dance halls, harmonica and blues guitar. Went to Paris, France, with Gordy Murphy's Revue Band back in the late Thirties. Nazi talk everywhere. I seen then it was always some poor bastards was getting it...I saw it was getting worse for the Jews and I seen bad as it was back home...well, I missed Warden and Strickland county and my folks. I was happy to come home."

"That's very impressive, traveling to Europe."

"It ain't much. You buy a ticket and get on ship and it takes you over there and you don't understand much at all but that maybe music is something everybody understands way below talk."

"What do you think of lawyers?" Jelly said and figured he might as well get every opinion he could on this day of wandering.

"I don't think about lawyers, son. Judges neither. Don't want to have nothing to do with them. You a cop, right?"

"Yes sir."

"I'd say that's close enough to lawyering. One thing them lawyers got on you is they make money win or lose. You don't make much lessen you taking something on the side. I don't suspect you is one of them officers of the law, are you?"

"No sir, I don't take bribes."

"I'm glad to hear that," he said and stepped on the stub of his cigar; he got to his feet and leaned on his cane. "Those Lovejoys was always a hardworking people. You take care now. Thank you for the smoke, young man."

"Enjoyed hearing about the old days. Maybe next time you can finish the story about the Russells and that case of divorce."

He paused and considered and shook his head in agreement. "I don't wanna dwell on the dark side, Officer Lovejoy."

"I won't mind."

"Guess that'll work…but that's 'cause there weren't no little old ladies around to get their ears burnin'." He tapped his way along the sidewalk toward the street.

"I'll be seeing you…" Jelly said, grateful.

Old Man Fuller cocked his head as if waiting for Jelly to say more and then pressed his lips together thoughtfully and began to whistle softly an unrecognizable old blues tune.

CHAPTER 13

▼

Fuller stood in the light under the tree and felt the softness blending with his own self. This rain today and that boy there. Taking the blind step into the blur of a crosswalk. Lovejoys and Russells. Lord, now there was a most violent blending of the elements, never for certain what white lightning might be born of inhuman design. Now that was near to Black Magic and that was something Fuller promised to behold at a distance. The rumblings were there again. He heard the talk. He bent now and peered back toward the Courthouse steps and saw the large young man moving in a river of light, like a wave of something going forth and seeking a destiny. Oh youth, oh youth, Fuller sighed and gripped his cane.

Sure enough, that boy was a glimmering of his ancestor preacher through his daddy's side. A mighty fine preacher, to black or white, didn't matter. Troublesome man for all these crackers. Fuller smiled and felt the hole in his upper front teeth, let his tongue play in the gap, sliding along his tongue. Come to think of it, old Preacher Sam Lovejoy was a blues man for the pulpit. He stood at the back of the church, Mount Olive, and fanning against the heat, he could see and better still hear that old man, waving his worn Bible, thumping that pulpit, tie undone, sweating, in the spirit…

Fuller closed his gray eye and felt the sunshine and listened in vivid memory to old man Lovejoy…that blues organ voice working the room. "Now you take, brothers and sisters, the Gospel of Mark…and at the baptism of Jesus by John in the waters of the Jordan, I am reminded of that passage in Mark, yes, where Jesus was coming out of the water, yes now, and he saw heaven torn open and the Spirit descending on him like a dove, yes and, and a voice spoke from heaven and the voice said: You are my Son, whom I love, with you I am well pleased."

And then came the dramatic pause and time and your personal eternity seemed to stand still, opening your heart with tenderness and welcoming to the unpredictable pain of living, of suffering, and the congregation smiled in their transport and waited for their righteous discipline. And old man Lovejoy whirled round catching everyone's eye and said, "And what happened then, friends, oh you know, that Spirit sent Jesus out in the desert forty days, and there he was tempted and teased by Satan himself…and as the Bible tells us, Jesus was with wild animals, and angels attended him, yes they did."

Jelly slipped into the back of the ornate grand jury trial room. He took out a notebook to take notes on any cases of interest. The state attorney Richard Hickock was a thirty year veteran and no nonsense baritone that carried to every inch of the room. The light was pale as the clouds came back through the town and rain spattered on the high glass windows behind the judge, the Honorable Henrietta Wright, twenty-five year veteran of the county bench. Clustered down front were the defending attorneys for the cases under review sitting with their clients out on bail.

The jury foreman Chester Peterson was a retired accountant and enjoyed his periodic appearances. He had a high clear voice that wavered under questioning.

In the first case under review the grand jury handed down an indictment on an HIV-infected prisoner who allegedly scratched and bit a correctional officer. A white man Turner Bellows, 35, of Valdosta was indicted on reckless conduct at the Flint River Detention Center. Jelly had heard through the grapevine that the guard was lucky. So far no evidence in tests that he was infected.

In a second case, Alejandro Vasques, 27, Strickland County, a trusty serving a sentence for driving under the influence and without a license, took a corrections vehicle and drove away from a ditch clearing road work site without permission. His trusty status was revoked and additional time would be added to his sentence if violation was proved. The judge hammered that one home and dispensed with further details.

Chester Peterson cleared his throat. "And finally, your Honor, we hand down a bill of indictment today on Taylor L. Johns, 45, of 651 East Cotton Street, for allegedly sexually molesting a boy under the age of thirteen between June of last year until September." Jelly jotted down his name…yep, old Tay Johns was in and out of trouble with kids…selling dope near school grounds, taking them home and getting them high and naked.

Judge Wright looked at Chester Peterson and then at County Prosecutor Richard Hickock. "I believe you had other indictments?"

"Yes we do," Hickock said.

"How do you find in the remaining cases?" Judge Wright said.

Chester Peterson glanced at the six other jurors on the grand jury.

"Your Honor, in the remaining cases we the Grand Jury did not find enough evidence to proceed to trial."

There was a stir of excitement behind the rail where the defendant attorneys sat with their clients and families.

"You are returning these cases as no bills?" the Judge said and raised her eyebrows at the Prosecutor who shrugged slightly.

Jelly knew there wasn't enough manpower to investigate many of these petty criminal actions. A certain number were cut loose.

"Well, let's hear them then," Judge Wright said with a touch of annoyance in her tone and nodded to Peterson. She tapped her gavel. "Quiet please down front."

Peterson shuffled his papers.

Jelly made short notes on the no bills. Charges were dropped on Edsel Smithers for aggravated assault on Tommy Hasting with a crow bar at the Gulf Station on North Morton Street, and also dropped were misdemeanor simple battery for allegedly kicking Manager Jackson Sales and also misdemeanor criminal trespass. Jelly knew them all and Edsel Smithers was a failed local garage band guitarist who basically took out his brain dead druggie lows on whoever got in his way.

No indictment was handed down on Benny Buddy Benton for allegedly making terroristic threats on Kelsey Carpenter. Buddy Benton was an enforcer for Floyd Jenkins gang, notably a hot-wire hotshot. Kelsey was a two bit forger and credit card scammer. Two vipers in a small box.

Finally there were two cases dismissed having to do with local Mexican migrants. One Jorge Modesto, unknown address, was not indicted for aggravated sodomy of a young boy; and the grand jury failed to find sufficient evidence for indicting Tito Ernesto Santiago of Frontage Road for cruelty to children in the first degree for allegedly punching his daughter in the face on Halloween night. Jelly didn't know Jorge Modesto but he did know of Tito Santiago for small time drug pushing...a real wise guy with a past that deserved more scrutiny. Jelly's partner Al Morris got a bad vibe off Santiago. "He's dark, man, he's seen some shit...be careful around him." Noted...Jelly circled his name and added an asterisk.

That was it. Round up the usual meanness. Brutal hands, uncontrolled anger, poking inappropriate orifices, petty theft and just plain stupidity. Jelly put away his notebook.

Judge Wright thanked the Grand Jury. She drummed her fingers on her desk and stared at Prosecutor Hickock.

"Mister Hickock, could I see you in chambers."

"Yes, your ho-nor, certain-ly," his southern baritone rolled off with an unhurried stretch of the vowels.

"The Jury is dismissed with the thanks of this court," she said and tapped the gavel and left the room.

Jelly knew she wanted to know why so many cases were turning out as "no bills"…a standard requirement and concern. And Jelly figured Prosecutor Hickock would sip a little bourbon with her and console her with the strapped police budget worries of this weary city and county and its inadequate tax base.

Jelly kept his seat and watched the lawyers and defendants leave the room. He made sure to make eye contact with Tito Santiago who smiled and tipped his faded New York Yankees baseball cap. Un hombre de muchos lugares, a man of many parts and a real macho, un guapo de barrio, a Don Juan…and a woman beater.

CHAPTER 14

▼

Jelly left the Grand Jury courtroom on the first floor and climbed the wide marble stairway to the second floor. Friday afternoon and quiet settling down in the old courthouse. The floors were kept polished and the wax smell gave the ornate woodwork of polished hardwoods a spell of an older time. Up here was where the famous divorce case came down.

As the family legend went, his great great uncle Lawrence Russell, a young attorney in 1904, was representing the young abused wife of Jebidiah "Jeb" Foster, the heir to the vast Foster farmlands of Southwest Strickland County. Early founders, the Fosters kept their own rules and disciplined their sharecroppers as they saw fit. Apparently the same had been true of their errant wives. And middle-aged Jebidiah, still awaiting his full inheritance from his father, was a frustrated man, chomping to take over the Foster kingdom…a veritable king in a false democracy. His daddy, old Perry Foster, was a one-legged Civil War veteran, cantankerous and mean as a snake. His enemies oddly ended up in the rivers, their bloated bodies filled with buckshot. No one saw or heard a thing. The city of Warden and the law were like a distant galaxy away from the Foster estate and its little railroad lumber and turpentine supply town of Heloise, named after old Perry's mother.

Jeb however, against his father's wishes for him to marry a local farm girl of good stock, had taken a wife from Peachtree Street in Atlanta…Sarah Ann Piedmont. Sarah Ann was the beautiful only daughter of a well known doctor in Atlanta; she had graduated with a degree in the classics from Agnes Scott College for Women; she had traveled to New York and beyond for a one year tour of Europe after graduation. She was by all measure a sophisticated, modern woman…and yet, after returning to Atlanta to take up a teaching career, she found herself pursued by Jebidiah Foster and his reputation as a strong man of business, a millionaire with an interest in world politics. He read the New York Times…when it was available. And he didn't chew and spit in cuspidors. He was strong, remarkably stoical and courtly in Atlanta society. She found him charming, careful and occasionally profound, with a glimmer of distant thoughts in his chestnut eyes.

Jelly stood outside the old courtroom, and taking a deep breath, eased open the doors. The dim lights cast a spectral gray film across the room. Upstairs in the gallery would have been the blacks, down here the whites. All the jurors would of course have been white men. His great uncle Lawrence argued carefully the record showed. The trial took three days to present. Yes, the marriage had started well. Two children, a boy and girl, inside four years of marriage. But Jeb had grown distant, away for weeks on business in the Southeast, he neglected children and wife and local affairs. And then when home, emotionally and physically abusive. He struck the children in the face with the flat of his hand; he bloodied their noses; he bruised Sarah Ann. He began to fear she was seeing other men. He put armed guards outside the house at night and while he was away during the week. Finally he locked her and the children into a single wing of the house. Their meals were brought to them by black servants.

His daddy, Perry Foster, on his peg leg, hobbled down to his son's house one day and waving a pistol ordered the servants to free Sarah Ann and her two children, the boy three, a girl one. Sarah Ann wasted no time in ordering a carriage brought around and she took off with the children for Warden. There she sought police protection and that was where she first met the young attorney Lawrence Russell who was a friend of the Sheriff. Lawrence heard her complaints and offered to represent her in a case of divorce. She demurred for the moment and only wanted to escape to Atlanta and seek the safety of her father's home and local political protection. Before she made it to Atlanta however, Jeb Foster intercepted her escape and sweet talked her into coming home. Things went well for a few weeks but then the crazy jealousies and abuses began again. That was when Uncle Lawrence received her letter asking for his assistance in a divorce.

Lawrence filed the necessary papers. Depositions were sought but Jeb would not allow Sarah Ann to be interviewed. Lawrence borrowed a friend's new Buick and came in the night for her and the children. As they slowed near the house, she and the children leapt to the running board and fell into the backseat. They left in such a hurry they brought no clothes or money with them. Uncle

Lawrence put them up with a wealthy widow lady in Warden and had them stay there out of sight 'til the trial.

And so the trial went on for three days. There had never been such a scandalous divorce trial of the rich in Strickland County. Nobody thought Lawrence Russell had much of a chance against the Fosters. But Lawrence built the case up slowly showing the madness and paranoia and weird acts of jealousy committed by Jeb Foster. His father Perry on the stand shook his head in consternation at the fury of his son. His embarrassment and fear for his daughter-in-law and grandchildren caused him to break down on the stand under Lawrence's careful dissection. Lawrence also had worked hard at getting commercial townspeople on the jury, a majority over farm owners. He figured the commercial class of town people would have a natural distaste for the monarchial pretensions of these old landowners. While they were waiting for the jury's decision…Lawrence it seems had a vision of mayhem breaking out in the courtroom. He sent his fourteen year old younger brother Madison running over to his law office to get his family's heirloom silver pistol with the ivory handles, a pistol worn by their grandfather in the Battle of Atlanta.

Jelly walked down to the front row and looked back at the double door. What happened then must have seemed like an eerie dream. For when the verdict came down that Sarah Ann and her children were found right in their petition for divorce, and further that compensation should be paid, unheard of in those days, the husband Jebidiah Foster drew a pistol and shot the jury foreman where he stood and then the bailiff…Then he advanced upon Uncle Lawrence who stood blocking his way to Sarah Ann and the screaming children.

"I'll kill you, Lawrence Russell, you lying dog, right where you stand," he shouted like some Old Testament prophet. "No man can have her save me!"

"She's won her freedom," Uncle Lawrence said calmly.

"Dear Jesus!" a black woman screamed from the balcony and collapsed.

"Nobody move!" Jeb shouted. "She's dead to me, the bitch!"

He advanced toward Lawrence and aimed at his forehead. "Move aside, Russell. You've gotten your blood money."

"No sir, the law has spoken," he said and clenched his jaw.

And in what must have been like one of those slow motion scenes from a Hollywood movie, at that moment as Jebidiah Foster began to squeeze the trigger, he heard the distinct cocking of a pistol hammer across the silent room, and turning just for an instant he saw from the corner of his eye, fourteen year old Madison Russell standing in dueler's profile position, arm extended, aiming that silver cavalry officer's pistol.

"Too little, too late," Jebidiah said to Lawrence.

There came a single sharp crack and Jebidiah Foster's left temple exploded in a cloud of bloody mist. He was knocked to the floor and began to jerk and moan. The courtroom cleared in a hurry. Jeb Foster was dead in minutes.

The bailiff and foreman recovered eventually. Sarah Ann and her children returned to Atlanta, and despite Lawrence's occasional attempts to maintain contact, she never showed a lasting interest in returning to Strickland County. Lawrence came to accept that and found his own wife. Younger brother Madison was a local hero. He enlisted as a Doughboy in the Great War and died in hospital from phosgene gas poisoning in the trenches in 1918.

Jelly stood for a moment in silence and felt a frisson of pride and sadness. In his throat was a salty metal taste, a sense of loss and an unrecoverable glory for his family. These were such low times of petty, empty heroics.

His cell phone was ringing.

CHAPTER 15

▼

Jelly heard Connie say in a hushed voice on her cell phone, "Have you heard about the burn victims?"

"No. I've been at Sammy's and the courthouse."

"The police have been here since they brought them in but I didn't know if you knew. I suppose it's okay to tell you."

"Of course it is. What's the big mystery?"

"That Georgia Bureau of Investigation guy and the Chief and his aides, they're all over here."

"Connie, who got burned?"

"I can't talk long. I'm in a nurse's aide station just off the ER area. We've got to med-evac these guys to the burn unit in Tallahassee. We're waiting for the copter."

"For God's sakes, who are we talking about?"

"Jimmie Lee Crown and Derek Carter. Burned badly in a meth lab explosion."

Jelly shook his head. "I went to school with them. I know them well. They run around in Floyd Carter's redneck drug gang. Derek goes by Bubba. They going to make it?"

"I don't know. They're in bad shape. We've got them stabilized for the flight. They're on morphine drip."

"Jesus, that sounds bad. Those damned meth labs are really dangerous…it's like working with explosives. Were they in a building or…"

"In a truck," Connie finished the question.

"Stupid shits," Jelly said, remembering them as school yard buddies years back. "Poor bastards, must've been cooking up a batch of crystal meth for the weekend market."

"I better go," Connie whispered. "They warned us to talk to no one."

"Who warned you?"

"The Chief...he said to us in ER, this case is under investigation, you're not to say a word about this case to anyone."

"You're not violating the law telling me. I am the law too."

"I know that, Jelly, but I just don't like the looks of those state guys."

Jelly laughed. "They train for that mean look. Men in black suits with death eyes."

"That's it exactly."

"Everybody's guilty of something in their opinion. That's why they're so glum. And if you confess anything to them, they'll have to put it in a computer file and one day arrest you and put you away."

"There's one more thing I heard that doesn't make sense exactly."

"What's that?"

"Jimmie Lee Crown had a bullet wound, in the forearm. He was telling the police about somebody shooting at them while they were in their truck."

"Did they say who was shooting at them?"

"No, I couldn't get close enough. The police pushed us out of the room. I gotta go."

"Thanks for calling, Connie. I didn't hear a thing about this."

"I thought you'd want to know."

"You did the right thing. This is just part of the drug wars between gangs. I'll look into it...We still on for tonight?"

"I hope so...but I may pull extra work tonight with all this trouble. We've got an overflow in ER right now. Call me about seven and let's see how it's going."

"Will do...you tell them you need a night off."

"We both do."

"That's for sure."

Jelly put away his cell phone, left the old courtroom and went down the flight of marble steps to the first floor of the Courthouse. Near the open door to the public defenders Tito Santiago was making his exit. They met face to face.

"Officer Lovejoy, como estas?"

"Not bad Tito. How about you?"

"Hey, anytime the law let's an innocent man go...that's a good day."

Charlie Bailey, the public defender for Tito, looked through the door at Jelly.

"Hey, Jelly, you make up your mind about law school yet?"

"I'm working on it, Charlie."

"Good man. We can use you down here. Two of us can't handle all these cases."

Tito smiled. "So you want to be the lawyer?"

"It's been on my mind."

"I think you make a good abogado," Tito said. "Put away that gun and start helping the workers around this county."

"What are you working at lately?" Jelly asked Tito.

"I got my bad back bending over in the fields," he said and stretched and made a pained face. "I got to rest this winter and see about the spring."

"Uh huh," Jelly said. "Looks like you move around pretty good to me."

"But the pain it comes when you don't know. Then I gotta lie down. Life's a fuckin' bitch."

"How's your daughter?"

"She's okay. Nothing was wrong." He eyed Jelly. "Tell me, what is this name Jelly?"

"A nickname."

"Jelly…gelatina…that's the sweet stuff in jars, eh? That seems like an insult to me. You don't seem like a sweet soft man to me."

"He's not," Charlie called. "He's always on duty. Hit the road, Tito."

Tito smiled a wise guy grin. "Detective Jelly Lovejoy…I worked for Bill Lovejoy…in his fields…he is your brother?"

"That's right."

"Sí, you tell him I come back next spring. We do business then."

"Maybe you better tell him yourself."

"You see him before me, I think."

"Maybe…"

"It's a small world, Jelly."

"Yes it is, Tito."

"Adios por ahora."

"Until next time…"

Tito put on his sunglasses, smiled and strode off, his cowboy boots ringing on the marble floor, his compact body rolling confidently. Back problem, my ass. Sneaky bastard ran his own drug gang for the Strickland County area and posed as a Cesar Chavez of the people, a real Robin Hood for the poor…while making probably six figures a year. A real agrarian mobster with friendly connections with the county farmers…including his own brother, mister libertarian himself, William Lovejoy. He'd have to talk with Bill about this. He didn't like this little cutthroat insinuating a friendship with his family.

Tito Santiago kept his cool. These crackers and their families. What was he thinking? Of course blood runs thicker than water in every race of peoples. That's for sure. So why was this Jelly taking the side of the law? Maybe to put on a false front, a tough guy; but he could be bought. And if he could not, then there were other things down the line.

Not that violence was a bad thing, no, it was necessary to keep the people in control. Without fear these pendejos would tell the whole world what we're doing. And not even the thought of that was breathed at this time. No, because this was a new business here in the cracker Deep South and everywhere were other alliances…old ones, between the whites and the blacks and the whites in power with the white gangsters, the redneck mafia. Oh yes, these white people with their pale eyes and thin lips and their hatred of Mexicans, their hatred of blacks, their hatred of Indians, "towel heads", they called them, running the convenient stores and the motels…he had to laugh at these idiots. When the drugs arrived, they all came together in a common cause and the pricing was right, amigo, cheaper and better than either the rednecks or blacks. Yeah, pendejos, you gonna find out who knows how to run a black market and keep order. People here didn't know what suffering was. Lazy and soft, this was a great fortune he had been given, this territory of Strickland, and he would not fuck it up. And anyone who got in the way, anyone who talked to the wrong people, anyone who stole from him, the punishment would be swift and vicious. That was what the jefes in San Antonio and Laredo and Juarez and Monterey expected, demanded. This was no fuckin' joke and respect must be paid. Jelly and William Lovejoy. Hermanos. The redneck mafia had their old connections with the police…why not Tito Santiago?

Tito paused and looked up at the Confederate Statue on the courthouse lawn. He looked like an old tired man, a defeated redneck, a man who lost his slaves and couldn't get over it. Well, he touched the bill of his Yankee baseball cap toward the old veteran…move over, hombre, it's time for new recruits, new soldiers, and a new revolucion por los pobres de sul…the deeper south would take over the deep south and turn these soft headed people into peons. These were people who sucked the tit of authority and pain. They liked to suffer because they were filled with sin against God. And there was money in redemption, amigos…

At the curb, angle-parked, was Luis his cousin, who drove him around. Tito was too poor to have a car, a poor fieldworker, with a bad back, getting welfare disability with limited means. Of course, he smiled, that was what made him of little concern for the police. He wasn't flashy and he knew how to be a humble peon with a family to feed.

His smart mouthed teen daughter Angela sat in the cab of the truck with her mother's face and her dignidad, her anger seething like a black river of trouble. Discipline started at home and this puta could mean a lot of trouble. That's why things had to be quick and hard. Her dark skin hid the bruises of his blows. Plus, she would not talk against her father to the white authorities.

He had things to do and he wanted her in a safe place. Right under the care of the new padre…

He swung open the door. Luis and Angela looked at him.

"De nada," Tito said with indifference. "They got nothing on us."

Luis grinned, "Okay, jefe, buenas noticias!"

Angela kept her proud look of purity. Her mother had that dark streak of anger and pride. But sometimes he felt his own mind looking back at him and that defiance scared him…for at some level, he would rather die than admit anyone defeated him. That was Angela too but she was not someone he could trust in the business. Not yet. Maybe not ever.

"Donde?" Luis said and started the pickup truck.

"Tu sabes," Tito said and looked in the rearview mirror at unsmiling, proud-lipped Angela between Luis and himself. "La iglesia, pronto."

CHAPTER 16

▼

Jay, age fourteen, an eighth grader at Talmadge Junior High, sat next to Jelly in the dark of the Starlight Movie Palace. Overhead the tiny lights twinkled in the velvet purple sky beneath which the ornate fairy tale like grottoes and balconies peered down at them. There were only a dozen or so people attending the matinee. Their little group was clustered downstage center.

Jelly handed round the giant tub of buttered popcorn and the tray of cold drinks. Jay leaned into uncle confidentially.

"The creature…he's got a really big mouth, ain't he?"

"Yeah, he's a gill man," Jelly surmised. "Must not like being out of the water."

Across the screen in black and white the 1954 film horror classic monster strode after the invading scientists and boat crew. The humans were a scurvy lot. Like pirates out for themselves. And they deserved this reversal of fortune. Poor old missing link deep in his happy home in the Amazon. The human invaders all saw a get-rich scheme.

"Yeah, he's a real mouth breather," Jay said. "I feel like I'm getting asthma or something."

Sammy heard that and laughed at the other end of the row. Next to Jay was twelve year old niece Tanya. She had her thick black hair done in a pony tail with a velvet blue scrunchie. She had a beautiful complexion and a rosy health about her. Jay was lighter skinned but looked more like his dad while his personality seemed more like his mother's…and come to think of it, more like Sammy with his interest in books and film and ideas. Tanya looked like her mother's side of the family, maybe with some dark Creek Indian, even black blood running through the old colonial Bell family line.

Tanya said, "I like his fingernails. Those are some serious claws."

By mid film the tables had turned on the human exploiters, and despite caging the amphibian lizard man of the Black Lagoon, he escaped and took a few useless exploiters with him. But now the monster had begun to fall for the bathing suit beauty on the old river boat. His primitive instincts were raging and he wanted the humans' romance interest. As she swam an underwater ballet dance the creature could not resist reaching out from the thick fronds to stroke her beautiful legs and feet.

Tanya spoke up again, looking back and forth between her two uncles. "Wonder why he's interested in this human woman…I mean there must be lizard women in the lagoon somewhere or there wouldn't be a male creature, right?"

"Spoken like a good farm girl," Sammy whispered. "I'd never thought of that issue."

"Really?" Tanya said. "I was thinking a whole bunch of other lizards were gonna show up and help him."

"That's zombie movies," Sammy said, "You're getting ahead of the times. Things moved slowly back in the 1950s."

"Oh," Tanya said and stared at the screen as the creature stole the woman from the boat and swam away with her. "Oh my, she might drown."

"They won't let her die," Jay said, confidently. "This is the old days, not like now on cable."

"You have cable out on the farm now?" Jelly said.

"No but my friends do in town."

"Ah…"

"They watch nasty stuff," Tanya said. "Playboy and Vegas shows."

"Wow," Sammy said. "I guess this movie seems kind of stuffy and silly."

"No!" Jay gasped, and realizing his noise level, "Sorry…" whispering, "We can always learn from the old stuff."

"You sound like a director," Sammy said.

"I might study film one day," Jay said. "Who knows?"

"Yeah, I might act in your first film," Tanya said. "If the money's right."

"Right," Jay drawled. "You gotta take the family discount."

"No way."

"Shhh…" Sammy whispered.

Here came the Da-Da-Daaaaah warning music, signaling the arrival of the creature. In his underwater, air-filled grotto he was trying to hide the beautiful human woman in her close-fitting bathing suit. His fixed eyes looked out at the camera with a voiceless plea, his mouth opened to engulf air that seemed not to help him.

In the end the scientist David played by Richard Carlson wins the day and rescues the gorgeous Kay. The survivors escape back to civilization and freedom from the Black Lagoon. The lights came up.

"Poor Kay," Tanya said. "She's gonna be a mess after this."

"Why?" Jay said.

"She's been handled by a monster, stupid," Tanya said. "Maybe, you know, she's been molested."

"No!" Jay said. "He didn't rape her."

"Oh yeah, how do you know? He had her down in his underground cave for who knows how long?"

"No, he never did anything wrong," Jay said. "He just wanted her as a pet."

"Oh, that's so gross," Tanya said. "Kay would have lost her ever loving mind!"

Sammy and Jelly looked at each other and laughed. Tanya was a kick. So was Jay.

"Come on you, guys," Sammy said. "Your mom will be looking for us soon."

As they walked out blinking from the Starlight, Sammy said to Jelly, "Kind of reminds me of us when we were that age."

"I was never that verbal," Jelly said. "Maybe you were."

"Oh we had our moments," Sammy said. "Remember the first time you saw this and you had that nightmare about the Ax Man?"

Jelly had forgotten.

"You must have been about twelve or thirteen."

"Vaguely," Jelly said. "Makes sense with that old story running around."

"Yeah, the gills and the webbed feet. Course this guy didn't have tools like the Ax Man. The creature's a little more prehistoric."

"Still not a big difference," Jelly said.

"Truth is I think there's a local monster just about everywhere in the world…" Sammy proposed. "Some kind of dark thing that lives between this world and the next, that missing link with our past. It's all very Freudian."

Tanya and Jay waited in the lobby with another round of candy bars.

"Oh man, I'm gonna be in trouble," Sammy said. "Your mama's gonna be hacked off with me about your dinner."

"We'll save it for after dinner," Tanya said.

Jay shook his Payday bar at the two uncles. "I heard what you said about the Ax Man. I bet he is related to the Creature."

"The Creature is from Hollywood," Tanya said. "He's a man in a rubber suit, Jay!"

"No, I mean what Uncle Sammy said…that part about there being a slimy lizard thing…half man, half beast…that's what our Ax Man is, right?"

"Yeah, but the guy everybody calls the Ax man around these parts," Sammy said with a professorial authority, "he was just a birth defect. A giant with webbed feet."

"Well, that's just my point," Jay said. "Isn't it possible our genome contains the primitive half man stored in our genetics and sometimes that comes out…you know, the amphibian is *expressed*. That's the term in genetics. Some body type can suddenly appear from the deep past…"

"Your turn," Sammy said to Jelly.

"Hey, I just buy the buttered popcorn and drinks."

"He wouldn't have a mate," Tanya noted.

"Well, then he'll could come by and get you!" Jay said.

"I'm not his type," Tanya said and winked at her uncles. "Our pheromones are different."

"God I'm feeling ancient," Sammy said.

"Ditto," said Jelly and patted his older brother on the back. "Let's go find their Mama."

CHAPTER 17

▼

Jelly dropped into the police station to hook up with Officer Anna Gomez for the community visit. She was in the duty room and in uniform. Connie was right. Anna did have a rather voluptuous full figure and Jelly smiled to think of Connie's jealousy.

Jelly waved to her and she smiled.

"Just a minute," she said. "I'll meet you out front. We'll take my car."

"Fine," he said and stepped into the hallway toward the back parking lot.

In the equipment room half a dozen members of the Drug Enforcement Team were assembling their equipment, all black for night work. Jelly leaned through the Dutch half door and got the attention of one of the guys, Earl Hargrove.

"You guys doing a bust tonight?"

Hargrove and the other guys looked at each other. Nobody said a thing.

Hargrove said, "You better speak with the Chief. We don't know a shit. Just getting our gear in order."

"That's the old attitude," Jelly said and winked. "Need any help, let me know."

"Detective Lovejoy," a gravelly voice called, the Chief's. "I thought you were going to make that outreach assignment with Officer Gomez."

"Yes sir, we're on our way."

"I just see you standing here wasting our DET squad's time."

Jelly stepped down the hall toward the Chief and his assistant, Captain Ellsworth, who was always with clipboard.

"Am I reading a kind of hostility, Chief? Have I screwed up in some way?" Jelly said, advancing.

"Like I said earlier today," the Chief said. "You've got two weeks leave. I don't need you meddling around. I want you on vacation...like your partner."

Jelly stopped himself. He didn't want to jeopardize Al's current job search. He looked at Ellsworth who glanced down at his printouts.

"Okay, I get the message. But I gotta say I don't feel that tired and I think if you're planning a big drug bust or something...you could use me."

The Chief pointed his index finger at Jelly's heart. "If we needed you, don't you think I'd have kept you around? Just follow orders. It's very simple...two weeks off. You should be thrilled."

Captain Ellsworth glanced over his glasses' rims and studied a paper. "Oh yes, you've accumulated more than two weeks, Lovejoy. In fact, almost a month and a half."

"Much too long without a break...I know what I'm talking about," the Chief said. "You have to learn to pace yourself."

"The Grand Jury returned no bills on another batch of felons today, sir," Jelly countered. "It's hard to take time off when criminals are getting away with their crimes because we don't have enough time to gather even the most basic evidence."

"Detective Lovejoy," the Chief said, "now you're nosing into my turf. That's not a function under your job description, is it?"

"No sir, not exactly although..."

"No no, it's simply an administrative political issue. That's between me and the budget planners and the city and county administrators. It's way beyond your level of expertise. Do you understand that?"

Jelly started to speak but saw Officer Gomez coming toward him with her car keys jangling and a face of concern.

"I understand, sir." He answered the Chief with Ellsworth adding a simpering smile.

"When you leave tonight," the Chief said, "leave your unmarked vehicle in the motor pool."

"Naturally," Jelly said. "That's standard practice."

"Let's make sure it is then," the Chief said. "Officer Gomez?"

"Yes sir?" she answered the Chief and pressed against the exit door.

"Detective Lovejoy is all yours now."

"Thank you, sir." She gave Jelly a slightly humorous questioning look.

"I'll expect a Community Outreach report on Monday, Officer Gomez," Captain Ellsworth added.

"Yes sir, Monday it is."

"Enjoy your vacation, Lovejoy," the Chief said, chuckling "I expect to see a much rested officer when you return and I don't want to see you around here 'til then. Understood?"

"Yes sir," Jelly said without warmth.

"Just looking after your health, young man."

"I'm sure you are, sir."

"What was that all about?" Anna Gomez said as she pulled out of the parking lot. She was driving her own Saturn SUV. It had started to rain again, the sky darkening.

"I think he doesn't like me because he sees me as a liberal officer, someone who's soft on informants and petty criminals. I made the mistake of taking the side of the poor as an explanation for crimes of property. I also argued the cause of legalizing drug use."

"Jesus," Gomez said and popped a CD into her player. A sonorous male voice began singing the heroics of a Mexican drug mafia lord. "No wonder you got sent out on community service. They probably see you as a social worker."

"Yeah, welfare worker and possible gay communist," Jelly said as a joke. "Tell me about the music...I've been hearing it around."

"Oh, these are the narco corridos, you know, the drug lord ballads. Very popular and controversial."

Jelly listened and tried to catch a line or two from the Spanish. "Good bye silver plated revolver, much esteem had you with my name recorded, with craft letters clinging here to my side, nor fear of government had you."

"Pretty close," Gomez said. "Not's so bad, Detective Lovejoy, for an Anglo."

"Gracias...I guess. So these narcotraficantes...these drug lords are sometimes seen as great leaders of the common people...like a Robin Hood, no?"

"Yes, exactly...fighting the Man. These gang guys are like the old revolutionaries. The people respect them for fighting for the underdogs and against the rich and powerful."

"Locally that would be Tito Santiago," Jelly said.

Gomez gave him an approving look. "You're paying attention then, that's good, Detective."

"Call me Jelly."

"Jelly? Look, I prefer Gomez, please..."

"Formal is fine..." Jelly said and knew Connie would be okay with that. "What are we doing on this Outreach visit?"

"Oh the Chief wants us to keep regular meetings with the Mexican community and he wants the new padre to mention him in his sermons and talks to the locals."

"Why?"

"Respect, I guess."

"Control too and intelligence from the priest."

"Well, if I know Father Rodriguez right, that sharing will be limited. I think confidentiality favors the communidad…"

Officer Gomez pulled up and parked in front of the one Catholic parish church, St. Matthew's, an old white stucco affair with bell tower. Next to it across a hedge was a small white house with construction scaffolding attached.

"That's the rectory," Gomez said. "That's where we'll meet him before his evening Spanish-language mass."

"Rectory?"

"It's the housing for the priests. The Anglo priest used to have another place in town of his own…but Father Rodriguez has no personal wealth to speak of…I imagine."

"He's from Texas, right?"

"Yes, the San Antonio Diocese."

"What do you know about him?"

"He's a friend of the poor, the migrant poor. A big advocate on their behalf…and he's smart and ambitious…so I think he sees this as his trial by fire in the provinces before advancement."

"That should bode well for the Strickland County Mexicans, then."

"Oh yes, he's definitely an activist. Come on, we're supposed to see him in his quarters."

Gomez knocked lightly on the front door of the rectory. A pretty young Mexican woman opened the wooden door and smiled in the shadows.

"We're here to see Father Rodriguez."

"Por favor, venca," the young woman said and turned away and led them into a sitting room off the hall. "Please, take a seat."

Father Diego Rodriguez came promptly into the room and took a seat opposite them. He was wearing jeans and a blue work shirt and a Houston Astros baseball cap. After introductions, he sat back and clasped his hands over his knee.

"You have to excuse me," he said with a fleeting smile. "We're adding another office and living quarters. We hope to bring in another priest to help with the work here."

Gomez smiled. "Things are going well, then?"

"Oh there's much work to do. The local population continues to grow with every agricultural cycle."

The young girl brought in glasses of iced tea and a tray of butter cookies.

"This is my new cook and housekeeper, at least part time," the padre said. "Let me introduce Angela Santiago, the daughter of Señor Tito Santiago."

Angela shook their hands. "Mucho gusto," she said.

"Much gusto," Jelly said and spotted a dark area under her right eye shaded with makeup. She gazed at Jelly and turned her head away and left the room.

Officer Gomez didn't miss a beat. "Her father has been helpful then?"

"Oh yes," the good padre said and smiled like a well-groomed lap cat. "Senor Santiago has done a great deal for us. This expansion is a result of his generosity."

"I see," Gomez said and looked to Jelly.

"Father Rodriguez, I don't mean to be impolite," Jelly said. "But I'm just wondering how he can do that when he's drawing welfare benefits for a bad back."

The good padre cocked his head. "Maybe I don't speak English well enough…but I mean in labor donated, officer. These men are collecting money for the materials and they have their trades which they are donating, you see?"

"Donations in kind," Gomez said. "Of course…"

"Is there some problem, Detective Lovejoy? I thought this was a meeting to find cooperation with my people in the community…"

"Oh it is of course," Officer Gomez said and gave Jelly a swift, hard glance.

Jelly looked at Gomez and then at Rodriguez. "Let me be very clear about what the police do here in Strickland County."

"Certainly," the padre said and smiled paternally, "I am always learning the way of South Georgia culture and its issues of public safety."

Gomez stared at Jelly with her eyebrows divided by a deep vertical worry line in the middle of her forehead.

"We have reason to believe Tito Santiago is a drug dealer with connections to Texas and the Mexican drug mafia…and here, locally, he's hiding behind his pretense to physical disability."

Gomez slumped forward and studied her shoes. The leather in her holster cracked as she bent over.

The padre's cheeks colored to a wine darkness and his black eyes shone with a fierce light.

"This is why you have come here today…under the pretence of talking community relations? This sounds like an official visit with criminal charges. Have you proven these things?"

"No, not officially," Jelly said. "I'm just warning you to be careful. Things are not what they seem."

"Is not a man innocent until proven guilty, Detective?"

"Sir, we have credible evidence on this man."

Gomez groaned. "Lovejoy...I think..."

"Further this man's daughter was abused by him."

"What?" the padre said. "Where is this going, señor?"

"The father was accused of beating his oldest daughter in the face."

"Why are you bringing these things to me, señor?"

Gomez held up her hand. "That wasn't my intention for this visit, Father."

"But look at the result," the padre said, his finger trembling as he pointed at Jelly. "I invite you here for a meeting of positive values and am now hearing a man tried outside the courtroom of justice. I must ask you both to leave."

The padre stood and pointed to the front door. "Por favor..."

"I'm so sorry," Anna Gomez said. "This was not planned..."

"No more for now," the padre said, "please..."

On the drive back to the center of Warden, the rain thickened and Officer Gomez switched on the wipers. Her hand was trembling.

"Listen, I'm sorry..." Jelly started to say.

"Please, don't say another thing," Officer Gomez said.

As they passed the courthouse and the confederate statue, Jelly said, "Let me out here, please."

She pulled to the curb near Sammy's bookstore and waited, the wipers beating out a slack marching rhythm.

"Look, Gomez..."

"Please, Detective, you outrank me so I don't want to say anything more to make this worse. Please, just get out of my car...and go on your vacation."

Jelly smiled. "Thank you, Officer Gomez."

He stood there in the street in the cold rain and watched her red tail lights disappear past the marquee of the *Creature from the Black Lagoon* toward the police headquarters. Street lamps were starting to come on and he was sinking into a world of deep deep granulated gorilla grunt, as his lovely curly-headed sister Lou Ann used to put it.

He did what any good detective did when he's the center of his own myopia. He called his partner Al Morris on his cell out in Arizona. Jelly stood in the rain and told Al about his day.

"All my warning signals are going off," Jelly said. "You know when you're in the crosshairs. I didn't want to disturb you out there..."

"Screw that," Al said. "I'm getting bored eating hotel food and losing money at the slot machine in the lobby. Let me do some digging. Keep your cell on. And Jelly…"

"Yeah?"

"No heroics, man, I'm not there to watch your back."

CHAPTER 18

▼

Sammy looked at Jelly and shook his head. "Man, you look like something the cat drug in…You ever heard of an umbrella?"

Jelly shook his head and wiped off some of the rain from his face; he settled into a chair behind the desk in Sammy's bookstore. "Call it a baptism of community outreach."

"Can you be more specific?"

"I'd rather not. It's a question of religious barriers and bluntness."

Sammy locked his register. "Okay, so you going with me to the hotel for dinner with Ella and Dahlia?"

"I'm going, yes, but not maybe to eat. I need to check with Connie and see what her schedule is."

"Feel free to use my ancient black phone, a relic of the Ma Bell days."

Jelly smiled. "I'll go hi-tech," he said and speed dialed Connie at the hospital on his cell.

"I can't get away just yet," she said, "but things look good for a bit after seven. Go ahead and eat."

"I'd rather wait for you."

"Okay, I should be starving by then. Do you mind if I skip the family get-together. I'm not much up to a crowd…I need a little peace and quiet."

"Absolutely. I'll swing by the hospital and get you, say about…"

"Seven thirty…if you don't see me at the ER entrance, come on in."

"Right…"

"Give my best to Ella and Dahlia."

"I will…"

Sammy pulled on his rumpled khaki trench coat. "Come, let us be messengers of good will in a dark night of rain and weariness…"

"So good to have a poet brother as my escort."

They went out into the rain, Sammy locked up his front door and darted along the sidewalks from store awning to awning. They jaywalked across the courthouse downtown traffic as dusk closed in and entered the lobby of the venerable old business hotel, the Hotel Strickland. Here for generations, traveling businessmen, salesmen, brokers, and politicians had stayed in staid rooms in the ten floors above the lobby entrance. The Magnolia Room was one of the better restaurants in town and here through the decades, many a contract was initialed under the watchful eyes of local lawyers and bankers. Beside the giant potted ferns that gave the marbled lobby the air of a Victorian era hotel, a signboard announced Friday night's Rotary Dinner: Honoring our Heroes. Speaker: Major Malcom Ardmore.

"This is going to be big," Sammy said. "I sent a box of *Crusade for Freedom* over here earlier this afternoon. Should pick up some sales."

"Who's going to be here?" Jelly asked.

"All the Rotary big shots, the Mayor, National Guard brass…."

"Chief Eldridge?"

"Yeah, maybe," Sammy said. "Are you guys getting along?"

"No comment."

They went in and found Ella and Dahlia already seated in the far corner near the broad window to the street and overlooking the courthouse square.

Ella and Dahlia exchanged cheek kisses with Sammy and Jelly.

"We ordered some appetizers," Ella said. "We weren't sure how many were coming."

Ella looked pretty with her full face and hair curly cut short. Her dimples were deep when she smiled. Always seemingly happy, she never seemed to suffer sadness for long. The opposite of Bill, the oldest sibling, it made some kind of alternative logic that following a depressive autocrat would come a generous, easy going woman without a mean bone in her body. At least none obvious to Jelly's remembrance of her almost constant mothering role as active assistant to their mother as they grew up. She now had three children, two boys and a girl, all in or near high school. Married to Jack Oldham, ten years older than her, he was a well-to-do grocery distributor to several counties and lived in an old ante-bellum restored mansion west of Warden in Heloise. Jack had a heavy drinking problem but he didn't let it interfere with making money.

Sammy jumped right in. "So, Dahlia, what's the doctor say?"

Dahlia shook her head in apparent dismay. "Lord only knows."

"Dahlia's got to take it easy," Ella said. "She's been working too hard. Anemia again."

"More red meat then," Sammy said. "You should try their steaks here. And red wine. French bourgeois food, my dear."

"I just don't have much appetite these days, Sammy."

Dahlia was about the same age as Ella and did indeed look like Ella's twin, except for her darker hue. She had a habit of tilting her head and looking at people in a gentle way. Sammy was right, the two of them together was like visiting a couple of psychic sisters. It would never surprise anyone to see them lay out Tarot cards and give a reading.

Dahlia and Ella looked at each other and then smiled at Jelly.

"Where's Connie tonight?" Ella said.

"Hospital. ER duty," Jelly said. "She sent her best wishes."

"I've been thinking about her a lot lately," Ella said.

Dahlia smiled. "And you know what she means by that, Jelly."

"I guess you're digging for marriage info," Jelly said.

Ella laughed. "He's the detective in the family, sure enough."

Sammy was sampling a plate of fried okra the waiter had brought. "Uhmmm...this is good as Mama's..."

"We wanted to have some things to remind Mama and Daddy of our old Sunday meals," Ella said.

"They're coming?" Sammy said.

Ella waved toward the window. "Here they come now."

And sure enough, there was Lou Ann escorting Mama and Daddy who were each holding on to an arm of Granny Rose.

"Oh my, we've got ourselves a family reunion," Sammy said. "All but Bill and Celia and their kids."

"I called out there this afternoon from the doctor's office," Ella said, "but nobody answered. So I left a message."

"Celia took the kids home to get dinner ready," Sammy said. "I think they're going to the Bobcat game tonight over at the high school stadium."

Dahlia shook her head. "Anyway, we didn't think that Bill ever likes to come into Warden, now does he?"

Jelly considered that observation. "No," he said, "that's like pulling a cypress stump out of the swamp."

They all stood to welcome their parents and grandmother to the dining table. In the function room to the rear of the Magnolia Room the noise of the Rotary

Club dinner hubbub was growing louder and somebody was blowing into a microphone. "Testing one two three…"

CHAPTER 19

▼

Amid the chatter of the family at table Jelly could hear Mayor Trout's introduction of Major Malcolm Ardmore, from the small town of Dinkins in the northeast corner of Strickland County.

"The Major will be telling us about his tour of duty in the Near East and with a special look at Lieutenant Jason Hollister's bestseller Crusade for Freedom. And by the way, courtesy of Sammy's Bookstore, we have copies for sale here at the front desk…"

Sammy winked at Jelly and rubbed his thumb over his forefingers. Money…He leaned forward and whispered, "Everyone profits from heroes…"

"Unless it's the victims," Jelly countered.

"Oh dear, I'm glad you're not before the microphone."

Daddy gave a prayer over the food, ending with "…and may God forgive us our sins of pride. Let us be happy with what we have." This was a little dig at Ella and her wealth and her habit of "putting on the dog" as Daddy put it in his secular comments on his children. He resented being treated to dinner by his own child, Ella, his oldest daughter; his farming poverty and his crimped retirement and limited means made him hostile at Ella's wealth by marriage to Jack Oldham, who in Daddy's unchanging opinion, "…was a rich boy drunk who had more money than common sense."

At the Lovejoy table the meals had arrived and the wine and drinks poured. Jelly held back from a main course and sampled the buffalo wings and cheese puffs; he also had a full glass of blood red burgundy and felt the stress of the day slipping a little from his brow. His Daddy was telling Ella and Dahlia about his battle with a wasp nest that hung in his garage. Granny Rose sipped her wine and stared at her plate of mash potatoes and chicken fried steak like it was an alien beast. Her eyes seemed larger than normal through her thick glasses and she blinked as if lost in the murmuring conversation. Mama guided her to pick up her fork and start eating, so when Granny didn't, Mama cut her steak into little pieces.

"Ella," Granny interrupted her oldest granddaughter, "could I ask you a question?"

"Well certainly, honey," Ella said and everyone listened to Granny.

"Did you ever get married?"

Ella smiled generously. "Why of course I did. I married Jack Oldham. We have three children."

"He's probably a good man like my Sam," Granny said.

"He certainly is at heart," Ella said, staying with the truth.

"Who's this colored woman?" Granny said

Dahlia smiled. "It's Dahlia, Mrs. Lovejoy. You remember me. I grew up out at your farm. Ella and me, we're old old friends."

Granny squinted at Dahlia. "Lord me, it's Dahlia. You sure they gonna let you eat in here with us white folks?"

Mama and Daddy looked annoyed. Daddy said, "Don't you worry Mama. They done fixed that rule. Years ago."

Lou Ann said, "I'm so sorry, Dahlia. You must not hear this kind of talk anymore."

Dahlia rolled her eyes. "I've heard much worse, honey. Don't worry 'bout me."

"Where's Sam," Granny said. "He loved country fried steaks with the milk gravy."

"He won't be coming," Daddy said. "He's got things to do."

"Such a busy farmer," Granny said and began to pick at her food. "He's probably down at the tobacco warehouse listening to the bidding."

In the distant Rotary Club meeting, vigorous applause preceded the Major's opening, disembodied remarks.

"It was my great honor to serve with Jason Hollister. We all knew he was keeping a diary. Lots of us did but Jason's was different. He told in his journal about the feelings of war, of combat, of the loss of his fellow soldiers, to injury and death…"

Daddy's hearing picked up on the latter and he cupped his hand to his ear. "Now that's a good thing to talk about. That's the stuff that stays with you."

Major Ardmore went on, "And to say that Jason was sure of his own heroic nature was not the case as he explains in his wonderful book. Thankfully he gave this manuscript of Crusade for Freedom to a publisher before he retuned to Iraq on special assignment…and that's when he was killed. A sniper picked him off as he made his way to help a wounded member of his elite counter-insurgency team."

Mama said to the other women, "I wish they'd turn the volume down. I don't want to hear about that poor dead boy while we're eating. Jelly, can you do something?"

Jelly took a sip of his wine. "I'll see what I can do, Mama."

"It's just fine," Daddy said. "We need to celebrate our heroes."

Jelly was grateful to escape the table for a minute. He crossed the long dining room with its scattering of business men and women and hotel diners. At one table with her silver-haired husband, a jeweler, sat Mrs. Flora Henderson, a librarian, now retired and still pretty; she was the first person to ever read to him…He was probably about three or four and she read Alice In Wonderland…and she had pointed out the key characters painted on the storybook walls at the old Carnegie library. Her bespectacled eyes followed him with a certain familiarity and he nodded to her and smiled. Put away that gun, detective, she'd probably say, and get thee to a good law library.

Jelly stood near the rear door open and slowly closed it to block the amplified sound. The Rotary Room held about fifty men and women. Major Malcolm Ardmore was a stocky middle-aged Marine in impeccable uniform. His chest was covered with medals and he hunched over the microphone as if this was the most difficult task he'd ever faced. On the dais next to him were the Rotary Officers, the mayor and at the end of the table, the chief who seemed busy making notes on a small pad.

"I had a captured insurgent, a terrorist, a man with a Ph.D. in physics, a very intelligent Muslim man, and he said to me, you are like the soldiers of old times, the Pharaoh's soldiers that came to invade us. But we fought back and we won because you have no heart for this place. This is our land, our rivers, our diseases, he said to me. One day you will grow tired and go away, just like the Pharaoh did long ago and things will return to the old ways."

There was a nodding of heads and a grumbling sound in the room.

"But I had learned something from Jason Hollister's heroism, his idealism and articulation of why we're there," Major Ardmore said. "And I told this terrorist, I said, look, I know one day this will be all over. Wars don't go forever. But let me tell you the difference. The Pharaoh's army brought you more of the old oppression of kings and pharaohs and dictators. But we're different, my worthy enemy, we're an enemy who will one day be your friend in your eyes…because we bring freedom and democracy, voting for elected people from all classes and tribes and sects to decide what you want for your society."

Here there was a big wash of applause from the Rotarians and a few whistles of support.

The Major picked up the rhythm of support from a friendly audience. "And this terrorist leader looked at me and said, no, you're pretending to bring freedom…but you're bringing the pornography of the West and Christian ways to replace our old customs of submission to Allah. You want us to overthrow Allah and become all-powerful like you and be the world police to remake the world in the image of America and Western capitalist values…everything is profit without concern for the spirit. You are the past and we are the future of the new global society, a new spirituality."

The Rotarians grumbled and moaned and rolled their heads.

The Major had made this speech before, his timing was polished, and he caught their wave of disagreement and rode it. "But oh no, I told this very intelligent man, we bring the freedom of religion, the freedom of speech, the freedom to write and publish what you believe. Religion is every man and woman's right to self-determine. Trust in your people to do the right thing. We're just the messengers of a better crusade than you experienced in the past. History and progress change and that's what you're going through…"

Sammy slipped through the half-closed door.

"Pretty good propaganda, huh?" Sammy whispered.

"The Major's gonna make Colonel any day now."

At the dais the Chief was staring at Jelly and Sammy in the rear of the room shielded partially by a palm. The Chief shook his head in disapproval and glanced at his watch and frowned.

"Let's go," Jelly said.

"Why?" Sammy said.

"The Pharaoh's hangman is watching us."

CHAPTER 20

▼

Granny Rose peered round the table and with her best persimmon face said, "I've been seeing that Ax Man boy, what's his name, the one did chop up the prison warden…"

Mama and Daddy stared at her. Lou Ann smiled at Dahlia and Ella. Across the room Sammy was leaning on Jelly's shoulder as they looked in at the Rotary Meeting for the soldier.

Mama drew herself up. "Granny, now you know that boy's been dead for years. Ain't no way he's still alive?"

"I say he's alive and well and he's a cussed haint in the woods 'bout my trailer and nobody cares two hoots to a whirlwind."

Daddy sighed. "Oh Mama, now listen. We're doing everything possible to keep you safe. I can tell you that boy is long since dead. You're getting Jelly mixed up with that boy…Jelly came by your trailer earlier today."

Mama said, "And later your nurse, remember?"

She looked at her son and daughter-in-law. "Where's Sam? Why isn't he here to straighten you out, son? You shouldn't be crossing swords with the truth and your mama's truth at that."

Daddy sat back and dug at his steak.

Ella said, "What did you see, Granny?"

"Just like I said, that big old boy with the webbed feet, the one with the bloody ax, he's a regular monster you ask me. And what's to keep him from chopping into my little trailer. I tell you I was scared and I couldn't remember nobody's number to call…"

"So what did you do?" Dahlia asked, concerned.

"I just went back to bed and dreamed about my Daddy and my first beau…"

"Oh no, not that again," Daddy said.

Lou Ann interrupted. "Oh, I can never hear enough about that first love of yours. Is it true you still have your letters…or is it his love letters?"

Granny turned coquettish, a tilt to her head, a transformative smile of demureness. "My daddy was a preacher. So you can imagine any man brave enough to court me had to know what was what. Oh, he was a handsome man…older than me by ten years…better looking than Sam. Sam I finally married."

"Well, you got that right," Daddy said. "He's the one tolerated your ways for all these years."

Granny didn't seem to hear. She held her head aloft and stared at the rainy street, the headlights with the raindrops falling and seemed to grasp something. She looked right at Lou Ann. "Of course I kept his love letters. Most of 'em anyway. Moths got the rest I reckon. And when I die you can have them."

"Me?" Lou Ann said. "Oh that's really special. Thank you."

"But not 'til then. I keep them in a special place only I know about…"

"What happened to your first beau, Granny?"

"Swine flu, honey. 1918. He went off to fight the war and got the flu in training up in South Carolina. They shipped him home but he didn't last long. I held his hand when he died. We were singing hymns and Daddy was praying for him in the other room with his mother."

"You remember it so well," Lou Ann said.

"Of course I do," Granny said. "Why shouldn't I? He was the first love of my life. But I was young and I had to go on and that's how it is…you just got to go on…"

"Then you met Sam Lovejoy," Mama said.

"Then I met Sam Lovejoy," Granny said in a strange echoic mimicking voice. "And nothing was ever the same."

"Did you love him as much as your first beau…what's his name, Granny?"

"Paul Green," Mama said with a roll of her eyes. "Grew up over there in Eastlake in that sawmill town. His Daddy was a foreman. They thought they was something on a stick."

Granny, ignoring Mama, drew herself up and looked around at everyone else at the table. "Where's Sam? Didn't you have the good manners to invite your grandfather to this fancy hotel? The poor man works his fingers to the bone for all of you and what does he get? Ignored?"

Daddy pushed his chair back. "Mama, you better handle this one, I'm about done in with her."

Mama shook her head. "Granny, Sam ain't coming. He's been dead for more than twenty years. Your memory's slipping…"

Granny with her gray, fuzzy irises and cataracts stared at Mama as if to hear her better. "He's been working awful hard lately. That tobacco crop has been giving him fits, what with all this rain…"

Ella and Dahlia smiled. Mama and Daddy stared off into space and Lou Ann looked toward the far door where her two brothers listened to the war hero talking about a crusade for freedom. Lou Ann wondered if Jack Turner had arrived at her place yet…the door left unlocked on the back. If she were there…he might be just now stripping down for a hot shower and admiring the fine housekeeping job Lou Ann had done. She closed her eyes and dreamed of a long sleep with the rain drumming on the old tin roof.

CHAPTER 21

▼

Chief Eldridge squirmed in his chair at the head table. There in plain sight was that Jelly Lovejoy, one of those legacy cops he inherited from the county consolidation. Him and his smart ass brother Sammy Lovejoy.

Come to think of it, the Eldridge's and the Lovejoy's had hated each other for generations since this county's founding. It was as natural as any hatred, what with land disputes and law cases and civil actions. It was in fact one of the old Lovejoy county commissioners that ruined his Uncle Norris' plan to bring a spur railroad out to Samson Heights, where not only could they have increased the family wealth with naval goods transports, but the junk iron business later in the years, the great supply that the Japanese bought for top dollar in their war preparations. Everyone profited from the war, even the poor southerners looking for an extra buck.

But the damned Lovejoys were a streak of trouble in their high and mighty ways. Who ever made them the arbiters of righteousness...what with the Russells when you add them into the blood mix, you got yourself some obstructionists of the first swamp water, yes sir.

The chief stared out over the local business men and women, the officials in the government in city and county halls, and seeing those two brothers back their, Sammy and Jelly...he knew in his heart of hearts there was no two ways about it. The bigger one, Jelly, the soft-spoken, wanna be lawyer...the bleedin heart nigger lovin' wetback hustling peace making sleaze artist. This was the kind of two-faced weasel who got you into a whole pile of horseshit. And that just wasn't going to happen on his watch. No sir.

Things might change around here in this county. They always did. But it wasn't necessary an Eldridge had to stand by and let it go without a fight. He'd worked too hard to make things run smoothly. Let the Mexicans come and muscle into the drug scene and god knows what else. Let the victims go down in their just ways. They deserved it and the squealers and brain dead dealers could go with them. There was a war out there every night creeping closer and traitors would pay the price.

He nodded his head in the affirmative and smiled slightly as he pictured the erasure of the Lovejoys from the local scene. The Chief turned his attention to Major Ardmore who was making a valuable point…Better to fight the enemy on their turf than on our own. That was the war on terror in a nutshell. Liberals were the slippery slope to hell…

CHAPTER 22

▼

At the table head Granny Rose fingered a stack of paper napkins. They were remarkably like her love letters. She should never have brought them to this hotel. Of course that was his hope all that time. Dear Paul...always trying to get her to the hotel. They would meet in the dining room and then...but she couldn't remember that part because maybe it never happened. Her father was a preacher. She had a reputation to keep and this handsome man had been "around" so they said, and she had to keep herself pure for the marriage night. From thousands of readings through the years, his beautiful handwriting floated before her eyes. She placed the letters in her lap and unfolded them so no one could see what he was trying to say to her.

Warden, Ga. 1917.

My Dear Rose:

Am glad you think of me once-in-a-while, for I'm sure not an hour has passed since I left you, but what my thoughts were of you. And if I could only get you to believe me and trust in me I believe you would some time love me nearly as I love you.

But Rose just remember this: That I love you with a love that will forever last.

And I will promise of all good and bad never to try to mislead you or fool you any way. And if at any time I feel that I do not love you I will tell you so. But I don't believe such will ever be.

And I trust that you will do me the same. But you must first try to love me. I feel like now it would be more cruel than death to know that you did not care for me just a little. And if our path on earth should part my fondest hopes would away. But here now let's don't look on the dark side of the matter, it is too dark.

It seems like a long time until the 21st to me. But the days will slowly drag themselves by. And every night I am going to say, "Well I am just one day nearer seeing my dear little Rose."

Here in the silence of the night I will take pleasure in answering your sweet letter. And it is useless for me to try to tell you how much it was appreciated, for the English language is too weak too express the pleasure it brought to me.

And Rose I would give the world if I could get you to feel toward me as I do you. If you did you would not have the least doubt in your mind about what I write you. But I am thankful that you are going to take my word until I prove to you beyond all doubt that I am in earnest about every word that I tell you.

It just don't seem like I can wait much longer to see your smiling face again. But I guess I can if I have it to do.

I am undecided at present about going back to school or the army. It all depends on one little word spoken by the only one I care for, where I go or not. If I go back I am going to stay 3 year and 4 months, if I live that long. I don't intend to trot back just because I get sick a little. Do you blame me?

I like to stay there fine only it's so far from home. France even further.

Well it was too bad about the fellow marrying after you had spent valuable time talking to him. Wasn't it? Well I've always said this world was just a "bundle of accidents." And if one half the people knew how the other half were living, the one half would have the others arrested.

My buddy Shea Johnson says, "This is a cold cold world, but we needn't worry about that...there is a warmer one coming for some of us."

Speaking of enjoyment, I don't have much of that these days. I amuse my self mostly by thinking you can guess what about. (You can't)? Why yes you can Rose. Of course you can.

And by-the-way I am dying to see you. I would give anything if I could talk with you just a little while tonight, (about 6 hours). I feel like I could talk to you that long just like it was coming off a phonograph record.

For you don't imagine how bad I want to see you.

This won't do to call a letter but you can read it over. And think "Well he loves me, but he is in the blues to night." No I'm not in the blues. I am like the calf the boy run over. I am out of chat.

Granny Rose fingered the last paper napkin...no letter, what in the world made her bring these durn letters to town where they might be found out by the common public. He was a good man...near finished the ninth grade before goin' to work for his family, wasn't it? He was always apologizing for his bad spelling, poor thing, but his beautiful hand always brought her to attention and a tear in her eye...

Dear Rose,

It does seem to me sometimes Rose that you do not enjoy being with me. And you know I am obliged to feel badly when I think you are not satisfied. But listen, I believe what you say about it more now than I ever have. I feel sure that you could not always say as you do and go on as you have if you were not satisfied.

You must agree though that you have given me some cause to feel that you were not satisfied for you have never been ready to marry.

Of course Rose I don't want you to marry till you get "plum" ready. If it's a year or more. But I do honestly think that you should say the time we will marry. And now if you fully intend to marry and you are not at all uneasy about changing then why should we wait any longer? But that's alright, just so long as you treat me as you have (most of the time) and talk as you do. I'll never again say any thing to hurt your feelings. You must forget all the hard things I've said. And always remember that I love you more than all the world and I do all in my power to please you. I don't suppose anybody has ever agreed all the time and never quarrel any. Though I think we have done more quarreling than was necessary.

Yes I believe that you care more for me than I ever dreamed you did. I am satisfied dear I believe I can understand better than I ever have. I only wish I was with you now to tell you this in place of writing. I'm sure you could understand better. But I'll tell you this and we can talk more when I see you.

It's all settled we will never cross again over any thing that I say. Are you glad? You said you would be. I'm satisfied I sure am.

I bet you are asleep dreaming some great thing. It's after ten o'clock. It would be "bedtime" if I were over at your home...wouldn't it?

Goodnight, Be Good and Remember Me As Your Lover Always,

Paul

CHAPTER 23

▼

Dahlia half closed her eyes and saw the early days when she first came with her mother to work for the Lovejoys. She had fallen in love with Ella and her sweet ways. They had played dolls in Ella's big front bedroom. Some days when it rained or the weather was bad, they set up a tea party in front of the big fireplace and made up stories about families and all the troubles they had.

Ella had such a sweet nature. She grew things in pots and old pans, flowers and green things seemed to shoot from her fingertips. Her mother said Ella had a green thumb and Dahlia kept looking for the color change every time they put together a new bouquet for the lunchtime table.

Ella told her things about the ghosts of the people who came and went across the old farmland. Down by Sandy Creek in good weather they built secret castles and there lived the whole day, with a pan of rice and a bag of bread and a jar of peanut butter. Ella said she knew the spirits lived in the creek and in the land. They would stand hiding in the leaves as her Daddy drove by on his tractor; he'd be sipping cold tea from a Mason jar and wiping his brow with an old bandana. He never saw them. It was as if Ella created a world that had a wall to keep out the evil things, the hateful things and the things that made people so down right mean.

"I'm as soft and easy as a puppy's belly," Ella said one day. "But I do hope I smell a heap better."

"Oh, you do, sis," Dahlia said, using their affectionate name for each other. Lou Ann wasn't born by then and Ella wanted a sister more than another brother.

They exchanged innocent kisses and hugged when they buried a dead baby bird.

"You reckon we'll die one day?" Ella said.

Dahlia considered the crude grave and popsicle cross near their hiding place at Sandy Creek.

"Yes, I reckon so," Dahlia said, sorrowfully, "but at least we got to be sisters before we go to Heaven."

"That's a blood promise," Ella said.

"I guess you're right," Dahlia had to agree, not really knowing what that would mean then or in the future. She just knew she never wanted to lose her good friend.

CHAPTER 24

▼

The restaurant was loud with speeches, with complaints from family, from the unrelenting rain on the pavement beyond their backs. Ella felt Dahlia's reminiscence and reached over and lay her hand on top of Dahlia's. They smiled and turned to look at each other.

I'm dying, Dahlia thought, keeping her weak smile with a wink of surprise.

We're all dying, Ella thought, but we don't have to be alone.

You won't leave me.

No, I'll never leave you. And remember, nothing is for certain sure. Miracles are everywhere. This…this communication is a miracle we share. The world of the spirit survives all this.

I'm not afraid, Dahlia realized, not in the ordinary way. Relieved maybe. Yes, happy to know my part of this story is done. It's been a long long time coming it seems even though I don't have many earth years.

You're an old soul, Ella reaffirmed for the millionth time.

Why are we here? Dahlia wondered.

Ella squeezed her hand and nodded toward Jelly and Sammy in silhouette in the Rotary doorway. Dahlia understood.

Mama was telling Daddy to cut back on his wine. He was emptying another bottle and getting louder and more aggressive with each upturned glass.

"Fruit of the vine!" he nearly shouted. "Jesus drank it, did he not, I ask you. Cleans the arteries, that's what the doctors say."

"Daddy, lower your voice, you're getting drunk," Mama said, turning to Ella and Dahlia. "He keeps a bottle out in the barn and every sort of hiding place. Thinks I don't know what's going on."

"Stop your meddling, old woman," Daddy said, looking at his oldest daughter for support. "I don't talk about all them pills you pop all the day long."

"The doctor prescribed them for me, Daddy. I didn't ask for them."

"That ain't what I heard. I ain't totally deaf sitting in my own house listening to you negotiating on the phone, wheeling and dealing with the nurses and doctors to renew your dosage. Oh yeah, old woman, don't be picking on my sipping…Sipping's good for you."

Ella thought of her husband Jack and his age old drinking habit, starting in high school, increasing year after year, 'til it was his life. Despite that he kept his businesses running, the grocery distribution, those trucks humming up and down the highways filling up the last of the independent groceries. And certainly when that played out, there was his Daddy's land, unfarmed by him all these years, leased out to real farming folk.

"A middleman…that's the smart money these days…neither producer nor consumer be…betwixt and between and keep the money clean, yes sir," said Jack Oldham, king of the hill, however humble the rise in his elevation.

Dahlia felt Ella's thoughts and smiled. At least he's a lovable drunk in his own weird way. Jack and your Daddy…

Guess I never cared much, Ella thought, long as the man is kind enough and leaves you alone when he's being his crazy self.

Jelly and Sammy returned to the table and the conversation turned to dessert and coffee. Lou Ann intervened to redirect Daddy and Mama to another topic, the high school football game and the bad rain.

"Don't matter," Daddy said. "Football ain't no sissy rainout game like baseball. The Bobcats will kick the holy crap outta the Cougars."

In the other room the Mayor Trout was shouting something about there is no freedom without sacrifice…"Honor is all about redemption through sacrifice," Trout concluded with an emotional choke in his voice. "I'm just proud to share this stage tonight with this great American…thank you Major! God bless America."

"And don't forget we got books for sale down front," a woman shouted out.

Applause imitating the heavy rain outside filled the inside of the hotel with a waterfall of foot-stomping, high whistling shouts of support.

Dahlia heard the humming of the tires through the night as Ella drove her back to their home. In the headlights so little was really in sight but just enough to make the turns and find their way. She could see that and feel the warmth of the car's heater along her legs. She would slump into the seat and doze as Ella kept things together and made her safe.

Ella squeezed her hand and brought her back to the dining room. Why am I troubled, Ella wanted to know. Help me through this, she said. I'm not so strong either. I thought I was but I am not. We will need each other. All the children and Jack will find their own places of safety but we have something new to invent. This is new for us.

Dahlia nodded in agreement. Lou Ann...sweet thing, she will be fine. She's making her brave way with that artist Jack what's his name?

Or whoever, Ella thought. Serial love affairs her specialty...flighty like a butterfly in clover.

But she's getting better...she's climbing the spiral of love, she's opening in her art...

No, we're here for Jelly, aren't we? Dahlia sat forward and gazed at him. He was looking at the menu for a dessert choice but his mind was elsewhere. He couldn't decide.

Behind him, in the middle distance, was a vague cloud, a darkness, an undefined trouble. A weariness of effort, an exhaustion of best intentions, a wandering, erratic pathway...

The always sensitive Sammy said, "So you know, everyone, Jelly's got two weeks vacation starting tonight. Wonder what he's gonna do with all that free time?"

Mama spoke right up, giggling, "Outta marry that Connie and go on a honeymoon."

Daddy said, "Don't listen to the women, son, marriage is their solution for everything that ails you...toothache to ptomaine poisoning."

"I got some work around the trailer," Granny Rose spoke up from her reverie. "And if you don't mind, Jelly honey, I'd love some more of them boiled peanuts."

Jelly smiled. "I'll get you some more, Granny."

"I can't chew a thing but I can sure gum'em to death," she cackled. "I'm gettin' ready for my bedtime now...somebody better get me home."

Ella, sitting next to Granny, gave her a hug. "Just a few more minutes."

"Where's my Sam, anyhow? He should have come too."

"He's busy over yonder, Granny," Sammy said.

"Bet he's got Bill doin' his dirty work," Granny said and squinted down the table. "Don't see Bill neither."

"Bill's no friend of Warden," Sammy said. "He hates coming to town. Says there's just trouble in Warden. He's out there communing with the coyotes."

Granny stared through her milky eyes in the direction of Sammy and Jelly. "I reckon I know that lonely sound in them long nights tossin' and turnin' in my bed. Lord, that's one awful sound…makes me wanna be drunker than Cooter Brown, I reckon…"

Sammy took a deep breath. "Well, that was enlightening as usual."

Ella felt the blank sadness off Jelly and Dahlia agreed. There was no time to lose this opportunity to cast a protective light around him.

Ella said, "Why don't you and Connie come with Dahlia and me tonight…stay with us a few days…as long as you like. Jack and the kids would love to have you for company."

Dahlia smiled. "Oh, that would be lovely."

Jelly looked at them for a moment without reaction. No, he shook his head.

"Thanks, that's really generous but I think Connie and I need to spend some time alone. Maybe afterward…maybe we'll feel like visiting you folks."

"Invitation is always open…to all of you," Ella said.

"Speaking of Connie," Jelly said, glancing at the dining room's old grandfather clock betwixt the ferns, "I must go or I'll be late for a very important date."

CHAPTER 25

▼

Been a busy day for Mister Tommy Edwards...and more to come. This rain done been bothering me enough. I want water this hard I just stay under. Down the lime sinks and underground rivers and caves. Holes in the dark earth where my soul wiggles its way to safety from all this nonsense on the surface of things. I been shut with that human stuff going on...Well there's no time to account for my bad taste in meals.

But like worms floating on a lawn, forced to the surface by the deluge, I find myself stomping through wet fields and grasses and trees. Not a thing to be done but spread out my wave of destruction. Force me to play a part. They're talking about Tommy Edwards, that Ax Man. And what do they know when they look in the window at night or the mirror down the hall. Do they see Tommy Edwards in the silver backing, permanently etched in their memories and experience? Well, that's a hope I kind of been thinking about far too long. And I do hope they're thinking of me 'cause I've been placed here for that special pure purpose. Pure, you understand.

Across the cotton fields, the cabbage acres, the pine forests for turpentine and harvesting for pulp and paper mills, they're eating everything as it emerges for their greedy needs. I heard the gunshots all day, hunting season in its prime. As in the old days, the first chimney smoke of cold in autumn and after the first frost, the men and boys heading into the woods to clean out the venison, turkey, pheasant and quail...and bird of peace, dove. Their warm bird bodies falling to earth, peppered and torn with shot. The dogs carrying them back to the owners, the canvas bag, the bloody bag, the heat of bird blood on the cold soil. As I lie in my havens, in my clever blinds of creek bend and cave, soft clay, orange and red and sandy like ancient sunsets, my eyes roll in my tortured head and I twitch in delight at the shots and the deaths, lives expiring, one after another.

But lately, now this rain, aggravating my nerves, oh yes, I have nerves, am I climbing forth again this day, and standing in the forest cover do espy these deranged children with guns issued by parents filled with love and murderous intent. And suddenly it occurs to me that as the twilight closes over this field of gunfire, that a swift visit of fate is at hand, and my work is fashioned for me in the great book of evil fires, that the great ones before me level these charges at me and all who follow to make the credit balance with the many debits. The great accounting ledger.

Over there, where the woods grow bare of life, where fox squirrels no longer survive, where neighbors complain of the unceasing warfare, my jarring presence is needed. We will put a stop to this rain of death and draw down a quiet for the swiftly folding night that takes us all…

There, a gunshot, and again, another…my work is calling me and I must not let these asides keep me from my major task of this night…so, my son, what is the delay? Let the ax fall and the crying begin again…oh, sweet pulsing heart blood, this meal for all ages…

CHAPTER 26

▼

Connie adjusted the hot water in Jelly's shower. These old farm houses with their ancient pipes and uncertain water pressure from wells far underground. Like their relationship really, getting older and the pulse of romance off and on again. And come to think of it, this had been going on since junior high school. Actually, she'd known about Jelly and had been watching him a year or two before they first dated.

The water was finally blended into a nice steady flow and Connie carefully stepped into the shower and let the blessed water begin to wash off this miserable Friday. Two burn victims and half a dozen other ER nasties. But burn victims, those two boys, oh my God, that was just awful. She reached out and took hold firmly of the snifter of brandy on the window ledge and let the water spatter the bathroom floor. She took a good swallow and put it down. The warm glow hit her stomach and she relaxed back into the rain of warm water. For a time she stood there and let the mood take her.

Jelly had this quality about him. She didn't know what it was. But she knew it worked for her. Her parents didn't exactly like him at first when she brought him home. Her father, the Scandinavian stoic, a quiet, strong, steady man, wasn't impressed with a boy nicknamed "Jelly". "It suggests spinelessness," he once said at the dinner table, just the four of them there, her older brother Gustaf, Gus for short. Gus laughed. "I know he's a Lovejoy and they're a pretty tough bunch." Their father grumped. Connie's mother, with local founding family ancestry, the Meads, had supposedly Creek Indian and black blood mixed in her exotic family past. Mother was a bit more indulgent and understanding about the vagaries of family blood lines. She laughed and said, with a wink to Connie, "No doubt the Lovejoys and Meads have consorted in earlier days."

Consorted. She had to look that up later that night and blushed at the thought that her family had exchanged sexual relations in the deep dark pine tree past. For a few weeks thereafter she had observed Jelly at a distance, a greater distance, making sure in some way that her attraction was more than this consort factor. Was he some long lost love affair in her family's memory? Was she trying to complete something, a circle broken in the generations maybe after the Civil War?

Connie heard music break through for a second in her shower rain and realized Jelly was setting up dinner, Chinese take-out, something they often did on Fridays, too beat to cook. The music was his favorite blues station probably, the one out of Albany, the birthplace of Ray Charles, as he often pointed out. She shampooed her hair and washed it out carefully, getting all the soap and conditioner out; then she washed herself from top to bottom, lingering in the warm waterfall.

She remembered her first kiss from Jelly. A seventh grade party at a friend's house and her friend, Julia Arthur, rigged the kissing game so that Connie got Jelly. They went on the sun porch that night, Julia's parents upstairs watching TV, and after a few seconds of edging closer together, Jelly had taken her in his surprisingly muscled arms and pulled her tight and kissed her full on the mouth...just like in the hot movies. And he had held the kiss and done it gently and warmly and without intruding his tongue or otherwise grossing her out. Even now she remembered her knees weakening and his grip on her lower back tightening so that their thighs came together and she felt his erection through his jeans. She had gasped and he had let her go.

"I guess we better report back," he had said, those gray eyes flecked with gold always promising some treasure.

She remembered saying something like, "How long has it been?"

"Not long enough," he had said and smiled and leaned in and kissed her again on the lips lightly. "We better go..."

That had started their love affair. And through the years, off and on, they had come back together for the same comfort of kissing and later lovemaking. While she had sex with a few other men while she was away at nursing college in Miami, she never really thought of anyone else as adequate. That was something she didn't want to detail to Jelly. Nor did she demand or really want any details about his conquests while he was away studying criminology in Tallahassee at Florida State. In some sense time had outrun their own professional working years in their twenties and Jelly was still working through the trauma of killing his cousin in the hunting accident. His brooding periods, his lack of constant commitment, were all symptomatic of this uncertainty. It wasn't until the last year or so that Connie grew increasingly demanding on this front, aggravating their relationship, causing these separations of sometimes weeks, even months at a time. She retreated to her garage apartment behind her parents' house. Her father had a slight stroke after retiring as a train engineer and she helped out her mom with medical issues. Her brother Gus was running a veterinarian clinic near Atlanta so that it was her main task outside work to help her parents. Her mother was a lively, earthy woman and that helped spread the load and lighten the mood.

Connie finished showering and cut back the water and listened to the music through the old walls of this ancient farmhouse, Jelly's great Aunt's home, probably in parts of it, over a hundred years of history here. She could hear him moving around in the kitchen setting up dinner. This was an old ritual for them. He was in his blue funk cycle and two weeks of vacation ahead of him. That didn't bode well. He needed company and she didn't have any time off, but maybe, she thought, he'll use the time to make up his mind about law school. She just wasn't sure what to tell him, but she didn't want to be separated from him for semesters like they had been in college. He was looking mighty weary after the dinner in town with his family. Clearly the police work was getting to him. He was even more miserable after she described the burn victims. In fact she had cut short her impressions and the dark looks of the police investigators, especially the GBI guys with their black shark eyes. She felt guilty just being in the ER with those detectives staring at everything the staff was doing to alleviate their pain prior to the med flights to the burn center at Emory.

And then to top it off, as they drove out of Warden, the delicious Chinese food from the Ming Garden redolent in the seat between them, he'd tried to sum up his confused impressions of the day. Maybe old man Eldridge, the Chief of Police, was right. Maybe Jelly was burning out. Or maybe he just needed a couple days off. In fact as they drove along in the dark toward his house, the rain letting up, their mood together seemed to lighten until they turned down the county farm road toward his place.

Connie sat down on the edge of the tub and dried her hair. She took another sip of the brandy, and then another. An ambulance had passed them going into Warden and she had said, "Don't even go there, baby."

"I'm not saying a thing," Jelly said firmly. "The rest of the night's for us. I'm off duty and on vacation."

But on the farm road the police car lights, blue, red and white, sparkled and rotated in the front lawn of the old ramshackle farmhouse and trailer of the Nesbits. Jelly had pulled over and rolled down the window of the truck.

Patrolman Jimmy Slater came over to talk.

"What happened?" Jelly asked him.

"Those two Nesbit boys…hunting accident. The older one shot the younger…"

Jelly turned away from Jimmy and he looked at Connie with his sad eyes, his eyelids drooping in stunned pain.

"Is he okay?" Connie said.

Jimmy Slater shrugged. "Winged him in the shoulder. He'll live. Lucky sonofabitch. Hell, people always calling in about those two shooting everything in sight. I been talking to their daddy and mama. The boys' mama and the oldest boy rode in with him in the ambulance. Their Daddy's up here on the front porch, over there in the dark…He's drunk as a skunk and cryin' and takin' on…"

"He never trained them right," Jelly said. "Gave them shotguns when they got twelve or so and let'em loose. It was just a matter of time."

"Well, he swears he's taking them off the guns 'til their older. I kinda doubt that, don't you?"

"That's a fairly good bet right there," Jelly said.

Jimmy Slater leaned in and cocked his head to check over his shoulder. He said softly, confidentially, "The boys claim somebody reached out of the bushes and grabbed the gun and made it go off. They say it was a strange smell out there, like rotten fish or something. The old man says it was that Tommy Edwards, the Ax Man. I ain't putting that in the official report. The old man's drunk anyway."

They had driven on to Jelly's place and he just shook his head and said not another thing about the Nesbit boys.

Connie dabbed a little "Heaven Scent" on herself and looked at her naked body in frontal view of the mirror behind the bathroom door. Hmmm…she wasn't exactly runway thin, never had been, but then she liked to eat and liked making love to a man with meat on his bones. She turned and looked at her figure and felt a certain pride in her full-bodied curves…Like the blues song said, built for comfort, not for speed. She smiled and slipped into her robe; then she pulled her hair up on top of her head and pinned it loosely into place. The brandy was warming her from head to toe. Now she was ready for a nice meal and whatever followed…mum was the word. Rest and relaxation were the order of the evening.

CHAPTER 27

▼

Celia bit her lower lip. Bill stomped down the hall. He wasn't going to the game between the Bobcats and Cougars. Tanya and Jay stood at the kitchen door looking at her.

"We'll wait in the car," Tanya said and smiled grimly and sympathetically at her mom. Men are tragedies, she seemed to be saying, way ahead of her age and maturity.

Jay looked a little confused but had the right instinct to get out of the house, get into the fresh air and follow through. He'd seen them fight before of course, and he knew his father was unpredictable in mood. What the heck? So he misses a game or two. I'll see my friends anyway. Celia felt a terrible sadness in her chest looking at her beautiful children filing out of the door.

She went up the hallway and tapped at Bill's office door softly.

"What now?"

"May I come in," Celia said.

"Sure, come in…"

She opened the door and there he was sitting on his desk with his binoculars hanging around his neck.

"Don't start, okay," he said. "Don't ask, don't tell…just like the military."

"That's the policy on gays. Are you gay?"

"Are you crazy?"

"You always go to the games with the Cougars, the school's big rival. I just don't get it. What's so important? I worked all day. I think I deserve a little time off. I was really looking forward to tonight…while you take the kids to town for the game."

Bill rubbed the palms of his hands on his face as if exhausted with explaining the obvious to an idiot. "Are you my wife?"

"Of course," she said.

"And do you trust me?"

"Of course, yes."

"Then I'm asking you this one time, do this for me. Give me the evening off from the family night at the ball game. I've got something I need to do."

"Is it something you can tell me about?"

He looked at her like she was deranged. "No, frankly it's not. Think of it as an experiment. I don't want to jinx my project, okay. It's bad luck to talk about something so new and uncertain. If it works out, then I'll tell you."

"And if it fails?"

Bill shook his head. "Well, in time I'll tell you what I was up to."

Celia stared at him. She'd been married twenty years and she knew her man. Bill was a strangely creative person and he didn't like acting out in front of others. He was quiet and secretive. He only liked to show people things when he was successful.

"Well, I hope it's worth the aggravation and effort," she said. "I'm going…"

He brightened and stood up. "That's a sport," he said. "And please, stay for the whole game, okay. Enjoy it…I'd appreciate it if you didn't say anything to the kids about what we're talking about."

"Frankly, Bill, I don't think they care…just as long as we're in a good mood. They're learning there's better times with other people than their own family."

He glanced at the window and at his watch. "I gotta get started on this little job of mine. Don't worry okay. Have fun with the kids. Call from town before you head back, okay?"

"What am I supposed to do if you don't answer?"

"Just keep calling 'til you get the all clear."

"Such a cops and robbers mystery, Bill!"

He laughed nervously. "Trust me, Celia, it's for the best."

Bill ushered her toward the door but he needn't bother. She was moving quickly down the hall. She didn't know what the hell he had in mind but she didn't like the smell of it. Let him cook in his own bad stew, she thought, town was a better place and the rain had stopped. The drive to town would take twenty minutes or so and they'd just catch the kickoff. Maybe Sammy would be there; she might just drop by and pick him up. Sometimes she thought she'd married the wrong Lovejoy.

CHAPTER 28

▼

Buzz, the tomcat, meowed at the back door and Jelly let him in. He went straight to his food bowl and began munching down. He looked like a small tiger and made a great working cat and mouser around his Aunt's old place.

"What, no hello?" Jelly said and began to sing. "The old tom cat was feelin' mean 'til he stuck his tail in the sewin' machine…he's movin' on, he's movin' on, he tore a stitch when he hit the ditch, yeah, he's movin' on…"

Buzz cocked his ear toward Jelly, then scoped out the radio. The music was good out of Albany tonight. A nice selection of old Delta Blues classics…down at the crossroads, Robert Johnson. Jelly heard the shower cut off and pictured Connie stepping out naked onto the old tiled floor. Maybe he should just slip in and dry her off…but something told him to play the polite domestic host. He arranged the Chinese food on the table, found pairs of clean chopsticks, and filled glasses with ice for tea or soda. There was hot and sour soup, chicken wings, chicken fingers, pork egg foo young, snow peas and beef, kung pao shrimp and fried and plain fluffy rice. This was an old ritual of theirs, these Friday night Chinese take-out nights. Some of their best nights had been started right here with the usual menu of food, drink and sex…and then talk 'til all hours. He felt ready for the full treatment. This had been a mind numbing, nerve deadening day. It seemed like he was on a whirligig that was off balance and swung wildly about surveying his past…from bad to good…but slowly descending really. No. This wasn't a lift into some kind of higher state…more like a sinking into a quicksand of paralysis. Like being stung by one of those blowguns in the Amazon. A slow numbing death…surrounded by the faces of everyone you'd ever known. That was what happened, wasn't it, when you started to die? All the people you'd ever know came parading through your consciousness…

Jelly sat down at the table and poured a Coke over his ice-filled glass. The bathroom door opened and Connie came out in her robe. Her face was glowing from the hot shower and her hair was piled on her head. She was wearing her fluffy slippers which she had left and she softly padded by him, squeezing behind his chair and in so doing pressed her breasts against the back of his head.

"Oh, excuse me, sir," she said. "Such a tight cliffhanger here."

"That's okay, I don't mind," he said and pulled her around him and onto his lap. He kissed her lips and held her close.

"Uhmmm…" she said after a few kisses. "I'm getting really hungry and horny."

"What's first?"

"Hunger, baby, and then dessert."

She let his hand slip behind the robe and massage her breasts. He opened her robe and kissed her nipples and sucked them gently. She wiggled her butt on his lap and he felt himself harden.

Connie eyed the table. "Oh, you've got the long lost chopsticks out tonight. Where were they?"

"Just reappeared. I don't try to explain these psychic manifestations."

"I'm starving."

She pulled herself free and sat down at the end of the little kitchen table and began serving herself on a large paper plate.

"God, I'm glad you're back," Jelly said and stared at her sweet, full face. "I feel like I've been lost in a stupid place for weeks. I'm not sure I'm out of the woods yet…but you being here sure helps."

"That's good. I realized the other day that if I didn't start coming out here again I'd have to buy a whole new wardrobe. Most of my good clothes and stuff are here. My garage apartment in town is like a motel room. I don't even feel like it belongs to me."

"Well, it's all here still. Except the stuff I've claimed. Cross dressing, you know."

"Oh right," Connie said, and made a face. "Very funny."

"You're just not my dress size though," Jelly joked. "I keep splitting the skirts right up to the…well…I shouldn't go there."

"No, you shouldn't. I thought you'd probably gotten a new gal or two and you were probably hiding my stuff from them."

"Well, actually I did, but they said you were a little too plump for them. They were all New York models. Anorexics. Skeletons."

"Skeletons for fashion capitalism?"

"I got rid of them. Who needs bones in the winter anyway? A man needs a full figured Eskimo gal."

"Well, I wondered if Señorita Gomez was taking my place out here. Guess she'd fit into my clothes and you'd be learning how to make tortillas for breakfast."

"Funny Swedish women," Jelly said, and remembering the afternoon with the priest, his face fell and he blew out his cheeks and closed his eyes.

"What's wrong now?"

"Officer Gomez has lost a lot of respect for me," Jelly said. "No doubt, I'll be hearing more about that when I get back to work after the next two weeks…if not before."

"Tell me more," Connie said and adroitly picked up a small clump of shrimp and rice with her chopsticks. "Can Buzz have a shrimp?"

Buzz sat between them on the floor of the kitchen and looked back and forth.

"Sure," Jelly said and watched as Buzz snatched up a tossed shrimp and carried it toward the cupboard room off the kitchen where his food bowl lay. "He's a neat cat really. Everything in its place."

"His owner could learn a few pointers on housekeeping."

"I'll let you lead the way on that."

"I'm not married to the guy. Voilá, I'm free of domestic duties. It's a wonderful balance…"

"We need to talk about that some time."

Connie froze, her chopsticks halfway to her mouth. "You're not getting serious and domestic on me, are you?"

Jelly smiled. "I don't know. Like I said, it's been one of those Fridays."

"Tell me about it," Connie said. "Frankly, I'd just like to get a little drunk and dance the memories away."

"We can only do that so long, don't you think?"

Connie put down her chopsticks and tightened her robe. "I do believe those law books are sobering the fun right out of your Friday nights. You better tell me more about what's going on…"

Buzz had reappeared and was waiting patiently for another Chinese treat.

Connie tossed him a bit of beef. "Now take five, Buzz, your Daddy has something to tell Mama."

CHAPTER 29

▼

The Drug Enforcement Team leader, Lieutenant Salston stared at Chief Eldridge.

"I've got my men ready," he said. "Anytime you say, we're ready to deploy to the surveillance hot spots."

Next to Eldridge in the shadows of the police headquarter hallway stood the GBI chief for Southern Georgia, Captain Ellis Browne, a longtime public servant. The Chief looked at Lieutenant Salston and then to Captain Browne.

"It's your call, Chief," Captain Browne said softly. "At least we are all here this weekend."

"Yeah," the Chief agreed, "and with this assault on that meth lab today...and those two men burned up..."

"It's a war...turf war probably worth untold millions." Captain Browne adjusted his tie and suit coat. "The drop in supply by the whites will mean the blacks and Mexicans will pick up the slack."

"And clearly the Mexicans are the comers with the migrant population growing on a permanent, year round basis."

"They're definitely muscling in," Captain Browne said.

"How's the light tonight?" Eldridge spoke down the hall to Salston.

"It's basically a new moon and we've got a lot of cloud cover. Shouldn't be a problem."

"Do you feel your men are ready to go?" the Chief asked.

"Absolutely. They're chomping at the bit."

"Good. I'm glad to hear that," the Chief said. "All right, let loose the night dogs, Lieutenant Salston."

"Yes sir, thank you, sir."

CHAPTER 30

▼

"You ever have one of those days where you feel like you're just wandering around in your memories?" Jelly said, leading Connie to the old sitting room where he had a small fire going.

"I assume you're being rhetorical?"

"Mostly...I guess."

Connie curled up on the sofa and pushed aside a pile of Jelly's law and criminology books. She tucked her feet under her and lay her head on the back of the sofa. Jelly poked up the fire and brightened the heat and light in the old room that now took on the look of a musty scholar's library.

Connie mused aloud, "Like it's one of those weird weather days where it feels like all four seasons are taking turns all day and night."

"Yeah, that's true. That weather out of Florida, tropical rain, with ups and downs in the temperature all day, dry then wet. I don't know. I felt all day like I was in a dream where I was reviewing everything. Even the Chief picked up on my mood. It's clearly decision time on so many levels."

Jelly related the events of his day, the morning with Snake and the Handel brothers on the highway, the drop ins with Granny Rose, his mother and father and the oddness of visiting his older brother Bill and young sister Lou Ann out at the old farm; then the visit with Sammy and Celia, the courthouse, the encounter with Tito Santiago, the monster film with Bill's kids, and the fiasco of the community outreach with the priest and Officer Gomez...and finally the Hotel Strickland and the family reunion.

"It felt like old home week, like some kind of summing up."

Jelly stopped pacing before the fire and sat down on the sofa next to Connie and ran his fingers across her cheek and then leaned in and kissed her lightly, slowly on her full moist lips.

"I love you, Connie," Jelly said. "I've been missing you."

"Really?" Connie said and drew back a bit.

"Don't be angry with me," Jelly said.

"Just what do you think I've been doing with my nights these past few weeks?"

"Go ahead. You have a right to be annoyed with me."

"Oh really, you grant me that privilege, well thanks a lot," Connie said and flushed with feeling. "You know what my parents think about us as a couple?"

"No."

"All smoke, no fire."

"That's not true and you know it."

"Oh, do I? You expect me to hang around while you go through this big exercise in career choice. You think this is the center of your life, this job future…"

Jelly knew enough about Connie to let her finish.

"I've always loved you, Jelly. From the eighth grade on…Never a doubt in mind that we were something special. But that's not true for you. You go around in and out of your next up and down mood…and I'm expected to ride this out, like it's the natural way of things. Like you're the temperamental one and of course I'm supposed to be your Mama and take care of you. You like having a nurse for a girlfriend because you think I'll always nurse you back to health. I'm just a self-therapy for you."

"Damn, well lay it all on the table, hon."

"I'm thirty years old. And the old bio clock is running faster than ever and gravity is taking its toll…or have you been so busy and self-absorbed you haven't noticed. I'm not eighteen anymore…or twenty-five…I'm working on the edge of exhaustion down there at the County Hospital. They're squeezing everything they can out of the nursing staff. I know police work is hard, I know it's dealing with the seamy side of people…but guess what, good or bad, beautiful or ugly, everyone eventually goes through the doors of a hospital and all that pain and suffering, we nurses have to share in it. Do you ever think of that?"

"Of course I do. I know that burn case today must have been hard."

"You ever see pink burned flesh, third degree, you ever hear burn victims crying and screaming in fear of the pain which just won't stop 'til we get the morphine in them?"

Jelly stared into the fire and let her go on.

"Jelly, I have loved you…and I still do…but I can't go on much longer. You and I have to face the fact of commitment whether you stay a cop or practice law or sell hotdogs on the courthouse steps…"

He couldn't restrain a slight smile. "Maybe Sammy and I could work a deal."

"I'm not kidding," Connie said. "Look at me. Look real hard at me."

Jelly looked directly into her blue-gray eyes. They were filling with tears but her voice was firm and steady.

"The time has come to talk about our future. You've got to snap out of this sleepwalk you've been in…"

"You've had fun with me, haven't you?"

"Of course, but there's more to life. Things move on. But I want children and a steady home and a life with a man who knows I'm here everyday for him. I want a husband who really loves me for me…not for my profession as a nurse, as a caretaker…You've had enough time to grow up now. You got a pass from me because of the trauma you went through with your cousin."

Jelly drew back. "Don't go there, Connie. That's not something you shut away in a closet."

"No, it's not. But it's not also a reason to let your life turn into a stunted stage of adolescence. You've paid your dues. It was an accident. They happen all the time. It happened tonight down the road not two miles from here. Those stupid Nesbit brothers. It was never a question of *if* but *when* they'd shoot each other. You should hang around the ER for a year or two and see how many things come through as bad or worse than what you went through."

"Don't minimize blowing off your cousin's head," Jelly said. "It was a lot worse for him than me!"

"I'm not minimizing. It's a bitch. Life's a piece of shit sometimes. But look at you…you're walking around carrying a loaded gun…you're putting yourself in the position of having to shoot more people. Did that ever strike you as odd?"

"Of course, I've heard the psychobabble on this before…from you and a dozen books and magazines."

"And you'll keep hearing it. Why do you think you want to run to the law?"

Jelly didn't answer. He looked away at the fire and studied the flickering blue red orange flames dancing up the chimney, the smoke twirling gray and vague into the night sky above the ramshackle old farmhouse.

"Look at me, please," Connie said and he turned. "Look around you. This old house is like a life frozen in time. It's your old Great Aunt's and it's falling down around you. Fix it up and it could be a new life, a new renewal…but you barely have time to throw out the garbage. You spend your spare time dreaming about an escape from your life as a gun carrying cop. But the only place you think you can live is either at the police station or the courthouse, cop or lawyer. They're flip sides of the same issue. Safety, law and order, saving people."

"What the hell's wrong with that?"

"Nothing's wrong with it if you really are engaged in it. You're not connecting…you wander around day dreaming about a life that might one day come to life. You're a victim of violence. You're afraid of it."

"Commonsense, isn't it?" Jelly countered.

Connie cocked her head and put her hand on his shoulder. "Look at me, Jelly. See this woman sitting here with you?"

"Yes…a beautiful, sexy woman who loves me."

"Exacto mundo, buddy, you've got it. A real woman who really loves you, but a woman who wants all her man…A woman who's been guilty of not demanding more earlier from you. Call me a bleeding heart, whatever. I didn't want to push you. I always thought with love and tenderness and patience, you know, things would unfold and we'd move onward into the next stage of life…marriage and family…and that you'd be happy to do that. But you see you can't enjoy those responsibilities because you're so hung up on your past…Face it, your cousin Henry Parker knew he wanted to be a doctor even as a young boy. You must have envied that."

Jelly looked at her. "He always knew what he wanted. I never knew what lay ahead."

"Look at it this way…maybe somewhere deep, you almost hated your cousin for being so sure of life. So much so you might even have wanted to kill him, unconsciously of course."

Jelly groaned. "Don't say that, Connie. Oh God, I never meant to hurt him."

"His death ended his certain path to a profession. Why is it so hard to believe this tragedy has blocked so much of your energy in choosing your own career and life path? You must forgive yourself to move on…"

Jelly stared into the fire and for a yawning, eternal instant saw nothing but emptiness.

Connie dropped her head and put her hands over her eyes. She sobbed.

Buzz strolled into the room and jumped on the sofa between them. Jelly began to rub his back and his hand met Connie's as they stroked him together. Buzz began to purr and rolled onto his back.

Connie looked at Jelly and their eyes held each other in a long embrace, their fingertips touching on Buzz's throbbing heart. The fire crackled and the ancient house creaked in a burst of wind across the neglected orchard.

CHAPTER 31

▼

"Sammy?" Celia said into the pay phone. She covered the mouthpiece as the football stands roared at some outstanding play. She couldn't care less at this point. Tanya and Jay were sitting with their friends in the bleachers. Celia was left alone and worrying over Bill and his odd behavior. Something was amiss.

Sammy's TV was in the background. "Celia…hey, what's up?"

Celia started to blurt her worries…but Sammy interrupted her. "My God, Celia, I better come over there. I can't follow all this over the phone. Is that okay?"

"Oh, thank God you were home, yes, please come over. I'll be by the concession stand. Bring a jacket…there's a wind and it's turning colder. Sorry…I sound like a mom."

"You are a mom and a very good one…I'm on my way."

CHAPTER 32

▼

"So it's fish or cut bait," Jelly said to Connie. "That's it, isn't it?"

Connie's smile and her dimples showed her sympathy for him. She looked beautiful in the firelight.

"I was never much for fishing metaphors...but well, yeah, we're at the proverbial Robert Johnson crossroads. And the Devil ain't getting my soul to make this happen. This will take the intervention of angels."

"You are my angel," Jelly said.

"And you're my little devil," Connie said and stroked Buzz who appeared to be in a trance of pleasure, his tail doing happy snaps against the sofa arm.

"Would you like another brandy?" Jelly said. "Or something else?"

"Uhmm...something else...I think...I hate being in the same old rut."

"All righty then..."

He went to the kitchen and opened the antique glass-door cupboard and began to examine his bar selection. The floor squeaked underfoot as usual with its complaints of his weight. One day he knew he'd wind up in the floor, splinters up to his hips and probably up his ass, as Connie had once put it. He chuckled and shook his head. Who the hell else really gave a serious shit about him? Of course his parents and brothers and sisters...but they weren't going to be there for the private times. What the hell had he been thinking? Just how long could he draw this out? He took a deep breath and felt a tight grip inside his chest let go...

For a moment he was staggered by the release of pressure. He leaned over and grasped the edge of the cupboard and tried to deep breathe through the moment. He was sweating and his heart was pounding...

Good God, maybe he was having a heart attack. He tried to call out to Connie but his voice was gone. His eyes teared up and he thought, oh my god, this is too soon…

The blur of labels on the whiskey bottles resolved into a moment of clarity. There was a pair of rings embossed on a bottle of Scotch, sparkles of light breaking out of the inset stones…diamonds of course. There it was, he realized, the next step, the slow-footed dancer taking the next turn of the waltz. Yes, even he had to own up…

And then he saw it in his inner eye like a childhood recovered memory…his great aunt Polly's wedding ring, long set aside in a special drawer in the old roll top desk. She'd put it away after her husband Theron died early into their marriage. She'd said, no, as long as I'm wearing the pants and running this farm, I'm not wearing a woman's wedding ring. It'll just get lost or I'll tear my finger off in some gosh darn farm machinery. She'd put it away and as far as he knew, never really wore it again.

Jelly took a deep breath and straightened up. He felt like a force had take over him and pushed him into the back office off the porch. He pulled open the hidden drawer and found the ring, a beveled diamond oval surrounded by six delicate sapphires.

He brought a tray with two shot glasses and a bottle of Tequila. Connie was in the corner looking at the old radio.

"You want to hear the ballgame results?" she said.

"No, that can wait…Tanya and Jay can tell us all about it next week."

"Sure…" Connie said and looked at the tray. "Oh my, I think you're trying to get me back into a playful mood."

"That's for sure," Jelly said and poured the two shot glasses to the brim and handed one to Connie.

She looked at the glass and held it to the firelight. "Beautiful amber color, isn't it?"

"Certainly is…but wait a minute," Jelly said. "Oh, I'm sorry…did you get the agave worm in yours."

"Oh God," Connie said and squinted at the bottom of the glass, a round object lying at the bottom.

"Here, let me take care of that for you," Jelly laughed and exchanged shot glasses. "I know a little magic about turning the worm…however difficult the metamorphosis."

Connie looked at him. "Sure you haven't been sampling. You look a little sweaty and pale."

"I'm feeling like I've just survived a near death experience."

"What…are you feeling okay?" Connie said with her eyes widening.

Jelly laughed. "What doesn't kill you makes you stronger, right?"

Connie paused. "You're not going to eat that thing, are you?"

Jelly made a face and looked into his glass. "Ready…"

"Okay, it's your funeral…"

"Please don't say that…" Jelly said.

They knocked back their shots and Connie made a face and exhaled a fiery stream of potent fumes. Jelly kept his mouth closed for a moment.

"Are you going to swallow that thing?" Connie asked.

He shrugged and rolled his eyes.

"You don't have to do this for my sake. Save your macho for Officer Gomez."

Jelly shook his head and reaching to his mouth, Connie turning away, he removed the ring. He rubbed the ring between his palms.

"Oh gross," she said. "What are you doing now?"

"Ancient magic," he said and opened his hands. "Abracadabra…"

There in the palm of his left hand lay his Aunt's wedding ring.

Connie gasped. "Oh my God, that's beautiful…"

"Miss Sorensen," Jelly said and got down on his knee, Buzz and Connie staring at the ring, "I know I've been a slow learner about love, but I do love you and I want you to be my wife…"

"Ohhh," Connie sighed and her eyes filled with tears.

"If you're not sure," Jelly said. "I can turn it back into a worm and let it eat my heart."

"Don't you dare," Connie said and let Jelly slip the ring onto her ring finger. It was a good fit and Jelly leaned over and kissed the ring and then rose up and kissed her on the lips softly.

Outside the wind swept up over the porch and the house creaked like an old ship at anchor. The logs dropped in the fireplace and sparks, like excited fireflies, twirled up the chimney.

CHAPTER 33

▼

Sammy drove to the stadium and on the way passed the old town jail that looked like a medieval fortress. God, the stories that old place held. Sometimes you felt the center going right out of things. Suddenly he remembered an old ditty from his childhood, because not only were criminals but the insane locked up in this dark edifice. As he made the turn at the corner and headed for the high school stadium he recited aloud:

> Rootie Toot Toot
> Rootie Toot Toot
> We are the boys from the institute
> We don't smoke and we don't chew
> And we don't go with girls that do.

He laughed remembering his experience living on top of a pole on the courthouse square right before college. He had to live in a small six by six plywood hut atop a phone pole driven into the soil of the courthouse corner, the southeast corner it was. That was how he could sit up there and stay up there for two weeks to earn a thousand dollar scholarship from the Exchange Club of Warden. It seemed like a great idea at first. The crowds were enthusiastic, the food hoisted up in a basket was reasonable, his waste products descending in a surgical-lidded pail. But as the first week ended, the disc jockeys fading away, the arrival of several rains and windy nights (at least it was summer before freshman year) battering the flimsy claptrap affair atop the pole, the really numbing pain was watching the world go by below him. It was as if the oddity had been accepted, a human atop a pole, a pole sitter…just another feature of the town and its life of daily rituals…and gradually he could see he was growing invisible. Few people came in the second week, even his family from the countryside found it too hard a trip to make. He didn't have a regular girlfriend or loyal gang of friends…so he sat in his airy dungeon and read Don Quixote and dozed in the heat and damp. His body grew rancid with sweat, his skin itched and his oily hair draped his skull like a plastic helmet. His teeth grew furry without cleaning and his nights were harassed by violent dreams, monsters in frightening mobs haunted the town and did unspeakable things to women and children. He would awake with a heaving heart and a sick stomach and would retch in his shit bucket. What price tuition? He began to wonder if he could make the final five, four, three…days.

And that's when he realized he was losing his mind. He was seeing people below as insects with deadly claws, their exoskeletons like their scarab beetle cars hurtling through the veins of the society, attacking, thrusting, intimidating the exposed, and the vulnerable. And that's when his heart first really opened for the people in the jail house. He could see their yellow lights on through the night and on the wind occasionally he could hear their cries and taunts and bitching and singing. And that's when he knew he was one of them, that the whole thing called society was a maze of rules and insanities…and he remembered that song ditty that he used to sing in passing the old jailhouse…a joke then, but now, nevermore. He was impressed that Cervantes had been falsely imprisoned and held for ransom; a man who knew long imprisonment and a man who lost his marbles and regained them by writing out the tale of the Christian travesty…the tale of love and forgiveness in grotesque human reality. And when he finished reading the old knight's story, he began to laugh and laugh…and for one whole night he stared up at the stars and laughed and cried and after that the final two days went swimmingly by…until like Lazarus in reverse, he was brought down to life again. He was a celebrity for one last day, his bloodshot eyes exaggerated by the flashbulb explosion of the local paper's stark picture standards. "Pole Sitter Wins Exchange Scholarship"…

Celia was waiting at the concession stand as promised. She looked exhausted, as if she might pass out.

"What's going on?" Sammy said and held her by the arm. She seemed to collapse into him.

"It's Bill. He's up to something and I really am having bad feelings."

"Can you be more specific?"

"Something illegal."

"Like?"

"You know…" she said and looked around her to make sure she wasn't overheard; and then she whispered, "drugs…"

"Meth labs?"

"I don't know…he's been doing something in the back fields on the farm."

"You mean back where Daddy had the sharecropper houses…"

"No, they're gone…you haven't been out there recently."

"I try to avoid the memories of those fields. You forget Daddy made me work the cotton and tobacco."

"Those curing barns…"

"Aha…so you think he's making drugs out there?"

Celia shook her head. "I don't know, Sammy. That's why I called you. I have this sick feeling in my gut. I feel like I'm gonna throw up. You know Bill would never miss a big game with the Bobcats. He and Jay and Tanya have been coming for years."

"Did you confront him?"

"Yes, I did…and he just said take the kids and stay in town until it's all over…"

"Until what's over?"

"The ballgame."

"And how much longer is that," Sammy said and craned his neck to get a view of the scoreboard. The Bobcats were tied, seven to seven, early in the third quarter. "Okay, so that means about ten, ten-thirty and then thirty minutes home…about eleven at the earliest, right?"

"I guess so…" she said and eased onto a folding chair. "He wants me to call first and not come home 'til he gives the okay. What if that runs 'til midnight or later?"

"Well, I'm sticking with you guys until you get home safely and if things don't seem right…you're staying over at my apartment. I've got a foldout sofa and a cot."

Celia clutched his forearm and smiled. "I hate to impose on you, Sammy. You're already doing so much for us."

"You're family…that comes first."

CHAPTER 34

▼

Jelly gasped as he pressed into Connie, rocking in his bed in the darkened bedroom. How many times he wondered had he approached this wonderful mountain of ecstasy with her…

And that quickly slipped out of his mind as he felt his energy merging with hers, their rhythm matching, her fingers around his waist pulling him deeper.

There was the release and the falling thrusts and her and his moans as they settled back together in each other's arms.

"Oh God," Connie said, "I needed that."

"Oh yeah," Jelly sighed, "doesn't get much better."

They rolled apart and lay next to each other looking up at the dark old ceiling with its thin boards, the lines running through the shadows like tracks into some lost land. They pulled together and kissed and stayed arm in arm. They were sweaty and naked and Connie put her arms around his neck and she played with her ring.

"Your great aunt must have really been sweet on you," she said. "This house, the land and all her belongings coming to you."

Jelly thought about that for a minute. The wind rocked the old farmhouse and the ancient oaks and chestnut tree out front creaked. "I think for one thing she didn't have any children…you know Uncle Theron dying so young. She became the farmer and she took in her brothers and sisters as they needed help. She was really generous and hardworking. Yellow dog Democrat all her life. Thought Christians ought to support a social net for everyone. Believed government should intervene for the little guy. And well, when I came along, I think I reminded her of her grandfather, somebody way back. Somebody she knew as a child…"

"And don't forget her final years," Connie said and massaged his cheek. "And you were always over here helping her when she was sick…especially that last year when her cancer spread. I was around then."

"Why yes you were," Jelly said. "And she always liked you even when my parents were having doubts about me dating a city gal."

"Don't go there," Connie said. "I hope to heck they've outgrown that prejudice."

"Oh, I think they've got bigger problems to battle now…"

"Like?"

"Like which pill to take this morning, noon and night…Age kind of takes the sharp edge off those old objections. Now I think they'll be glad to hear I'm getting married to a smart woman…and with timely medical information."

Connie drew closer and pressed up against Jelly and kissed him. "Small price to pay for getting their baby boy."

Jelly returned the kiss and wrapped his legs around Connie. Under the covers, their combined heat made him glow with a grateful joy. "Before she died Great Aunt Polly showed me where she'd hidden her wedding ring. She told me, now Jelly, you can use it for college…or if you wish, you can give it to the girl of your dreams. It was handed down from Theron's grandmother. So it's really an heirloom from around the Civil War."

"What did you say to her?"

"I thanked her of course but, well, got to be honest, it kinda creeped me out…a wedding ring that old. I thought it might be haunted with all the troubles down through the years. And then there was that something in me that wanted to do it myself, you know, scrimp and save and buy something bright, new and shiny at the strip mall."

"Oh come on, really?"

"Well, yeah…something untouched. Brand new. No history. I didn't think you'd like some old family thing."

"You immediately thought of me alone?" Connie said, a little breathlessly.

Jelly laughed. "Well, there were several other girls but their fingers didn't fit."

Connie pulled his nose. "Bad boy."

"Aunt Polly thought of it as having a chance to fulfill its mission as a love symbol. I think that's what she wanted for it. You know, she wanted the act two and three of her marriage to happen for me. I kind of thought it was a bad luck ring 'cause Uncle Theron died so young, chopped short. I didn't want that to happen to me...or to us."

Connie put the ring between their faces and in the dim light of the bedroom the diamond seemed to glow with a faint purplish light.

"Are you spooked by it?" Jelly said.

"I go with my intuition," Connie said, "and I loved your Aunt Polly. I liked her toughness and her common sense. She had a practical, thrifty intelligence but she also believed in doing good things for people. I never heard her whine or complain about her life. I just remember that strong laughter from the front porch when we'd come out here in your folk's car in high school."

"She thought you were special, and I think she had a good sense of matchmaking like Ella. Ella left the house when she was just eighteen and married."

"And Lou Ann was too much a free spirit," Connie said. "And Bill got the farm."

"When I was little she liked to have me over to watch TV...she liked discussing politics. She was a really smart woman. She was controversial too. Once she got tired of hearing Daddy's drunken racist, anti-feminist remarks and she piped up and said...well, might just be God's black and a woman to boot."

Connie laughed. "And what did your Daddy say?"

"He was stunned. He sat there a minute and stared at her and shook his head and finally said, well, guess I'll be going straight to hell then. Aunt Polly got a laugh from that one. We all did."

"That's why I'm keeping it," Connie said. "Strong women need to stick together. It's a long, long road building and keeping families together."

"Are you ready for that rocky road with me?" Jelly asked.

Connie smiled and twirled the ring once slowly around her finger. "I do believe I'm up to the task, Detective Lovejoy. Is this where you bring out your handcuffs and take me prisoner for life?"

"Now that's kinda kinky and sexy," Jelly said and rolled on top of her. "Marriage is a kind of lifer's bondage."

"And we have a lot of planning to do," Connie said.

"Oh no, not tonight. Next week maybe...but I want you to take some time off and we can go on a little vacation somewhere. What do you say? A little honeymoon prelude?"

"Not fishing or hunting okay?"

"Someplace quiet and romantic," Jelly said. "A rustic place in the country with a nice fireplace and good food..."

"Oh, I hear where this is headed. No sir, we've got to pack a bag and get out of Strickland County, mister romance…"

Jelly laughed.

Connie tightened under him. "What's that by the window?"

Jelly rolled off Connie and raised his head in a partial sit up.

"Right there," Connie said and pointed to the middle square of the windows opening over the front porch.

Jelly sat up and stared. The curtain moved slightly and he got a profile of two pointed ears twitching over the old chest parked under the windows.

"Why that's Buzz," Jelly said and felt his neck hair tickle.

"Oh, it's just Buzz," Connie said. "Come 'ere, Buzzy."

But Buzz didn't come. He turned his big striped head briefly, then tensed and looked outside again, his tail whipping back and forth.

"Shhh…" Jelly said and slipped out of bed, the cool room air hitting his naked body still damp with lovemaking. "He sees something out there. Lie still."

Just then Jelly's cell phone started playing, breaking the stillness, with a hurried version of "Take me out to the Ball Game".

Connie whispered, "Do you have to answer that?"

Jelly hesitated. "Yes, I better, hon. There's a lot going on tonight."

"Damn it," she cursed and pulled the pillow over her head.

CHAPTER 35

▼

For Buzz there was no reality like the humans in the room, this protected maze of boxes. He sat at the window and felt his claws in their sheaths stretch forward where they caught on the old wood of the chest. This man Jelly was leaning forward now while talking into his hand and slipping closer to the window. There was something about this man that made him seem like a cat, the way he moved low to the ground and the way his head darted behind the curtains to look out on the porch.

For Buzz, that sound name that came his way with all sorts of consequences, food, an exit, a call, a head rub or just a firm push this way and that…that name sound made him turn and see the woman staring at Jelly and himself, as they crouched together by the window. Buzz flicked his tail. The thing that was there before was gone. Maybe around the corner into the dark but he still felt the flow of energy and it was a human presence like all the other ones he knew. It was a young human like Jelly and the woman…he knew the woman and liked her, she was kind and liked to rub him on his head and back and belly and pull his tail slowly into a straight line of energy that made his eyes widen and his tongue draw back into the beginning of a purr.

In the early mind of his life, his fear place, he was picked from his warm mother and her litter and swept high in the air, whatever that was, and carried into cold night high over the farm of his birth, and with wings outstretched against the moon and the spectral light, his neck bleeding from the talons, the pain throbbing through his body, he mewed as loudly as he knew and looked out at the farmhouses and fields and ponds and copses of pines and he had nothing above him but the hooked beak in his neck and the large golden eyes of the bird, the giant bird, that later he came to know as an owl, a great horned owl, that lived in the farmer's tool shed that leaned over to the ground.

And in the faint memory Buzz still maintained of his arrival he felt the bird falling and he swung up with his free paws and scratched at its great big eyes and the bird blinked madly and flipped over and Buzz fell and fell and tumbled into a thick bush and bounced onto the grass by this very farmhouse. And in seconds this voice and man called Jelly was there and shaking a fist against the owl and the sky. Buzz felt a purr coming on and watched as Jelly slipped into his clothes while talking into his hand.

There were other things that walked around the old farmhouse day and night. And one of those was that strange tall man that was not a man that came in the night usually and stood looking in the windows at the humans. He walked with a dragging noise like a hurt animal. Buzz wondered if he could finish him off for Jelly but the warmth of the winter fire kept him inside where he felt safe from the other animals and beings that flirted through the farmland, friend and foe, and he knew too that this was not like the others, that in some sense, like some animals like the possum, there was no threat meant from these night creatures that passed through the silver shadows of moonlight dancing under the sycamore tree near the road.

For now, Buzz stayed put on the squeaky old chest and its musky smells and cocked his head for a better night view of the dangers outside these walls with eyes to the bigger world.

Jelly rubbed Buzz's head and whispered, "Good ol' attack cat. That's a good boy."

He grabbed the cell phone off his dresser and snapped it on.

"Speak…"

Jelly heard the familiar baritone, "Hey, it's Al."

"What you find out?"

"I called the dispatcher in Warden, right?"

"Yeah."

"She owes me a favor or two. I helped her teenager out of a drug charge."

"Okay," Jelly said softly.

"Why you whispering, man? Where are you?"

"I'm at home and I think there's somebody outside the house."

Connie sat up. "What's going on?"

Jelly waved his hand to lie down.

"Oh my god," Connie said. "I'm marrying a cop…what should I expect!"

"Is that Connie?" Al said.

"Of course," Jelly said. "Who else?"

"I ain't going there, partner."

"So what did you learn from the dispatcher…that's Officer Bingham, right?"

"Exactly," Al said. "She said they're staking out several hot spots this Friday night…already dispersed by now and in position."

"Missing the big Bobcat-Cougar showdown. That must've been a sacrifice for the guys."

"Yeah, no shit," Al said. "Hey and she also said the GBI's moving into the department big time on some kind of an investigation into corruption. They've got all our bank accounts red-flagged to see if we're making any big deposits."

"Bribes from the drug gangs, right?"

"Yep, you got it. Standard practice for the GBI."

"Well, they'll see what kind of shit pay we're making, won't they?"

"You got that right," Al said and laughed.

"What else?" Jelly said. "What about this new priest in town. Anything?"

Now Al was whispering. "I had to go through the Flagstaff office but they had good contacts with Texas and the border gang reports. And you won't believe this…"

"Try me…I'm beginning to believe just about anything can happen today."

"Your Padre there, Father Diego Rodriguez…this is really kinky, man, he's got a twin brother in the Monterey drug cartel and it was through this cartel's influence that the good Father got sent to Southwest Georgia, especially at the request of one…guess who?"

"Tito Santiago."

"Bingo. You got it. Turns out Tito is no two bit player or distributor. He's like a lead marketer for the cartel. He gets sent to open new markets and then reappears in the next target area, new name and identity. He's a bad ass dude. El Paso police and the FBI believe he's an enforcer. A gang of guys who choked up evidence two years ago about their advance into the Mississippi Delta were slaughtered, them and their kids, professional hits."

"I remember that case. That's the Reconquista argument, right?"

"Exactly, these guys consider it a political-economic war too…taking over the U.S. and there are certain influential Mexicans who see it as legitimate. They look the other way."

"What else you got?" Jelly asked and pulled on his boots. "I gotta see who's sneaking around the place."

"Godammit, Jelly," Al hissed under his breath, "I should be there with you. Lay low and don't take no chances."

"I'm afraid that's a little late now, Al. I got a bad feeling my brother Bill might be mixed up in this. The signs have been coming in all day and I didn't want to face it."

"Mister Libertarian back-to-the-soil hard ass?"

"Yeah, well I hope not…but I gotta follow this out. By the way, thanks for the research. Wish you were here. You and Suzie could join us for a drink…Connie's accepted my engagement offer tonight."

"Man, that's great!" Al said. "Suzie will be thrilled to hear that. She's down at the pool with the kids."

"I gotta run, Al," Jelly said and paused half a beat, "wish you were here."

"Jelly, about that stranger out there in the dark…my hunch is you're under surveillance by the DET…our guys…or maybe Tito's gang. Either way, be fuckin' careful when you stick your head out that front door."

"Ain't going out the front door, buddy. Got another plan."

"Holy shit…you call me back when this is all over. No matter what time of day or night. Goddammit! I knew I shouldn't have left town when I did."

"Screw that," Jelly said. "You got a wife and kids. I'll be in touch…and Al…"

"Yeah?"

"Thanks, man…"

"Go get'em, buddy…and put on that protective vest before you sling any lead. Hear me?"

"I hear you."

CHAPTER 36

▼

Jelly went to the far end of the old house and opened up a storage room no longer safe enough for weight bearing. The floor had once had a chute to the outside. Over the hole was a sheet of corrugated tin. He carefully and quietly slid it off the hole and dropped down under the house and sat in a squat for a second, letting his eyes adjust to the dark.

He heard Connie moving around in the front room. She was dressing and getting ready to exit the premises at his signal. Depending on the situation they would have several alternatives...some he didn't want to think about...like heading for the woods and the pond down below the creek. From there he knew back trails to his Daddy's farmland a few miles distant. But that wasn't going to be an option, not with a gun and a truck and a bullet proof vest. He tapped his chest protector and duck walked out from under the back end of the rear porch and stood up in the dark shadow of the kitchen.

Moving back across his aunt's former chicken yards and then down the garden wire beyond the pecan grove, he hit the fence parallel to the county-maintained road. From there he bent double and ran along the inside of his kudzu vine at a slow trot, stopping and listening, then moving ahead again. If anyone wanted to hide a vehicle and still keep infrared binoculars focused on his place, it was likely to be his farmer neighbor Sly Slocomb's dirt road down to his cattle and horse feeding and watering station. Sly was a little lazy so he'd linked up a portable radio to the wiring to the water pump; that way he could just pull off the highway and roll down his truck window to hear if the water pump was still running. The AM radio played country and western music, twenty four hours, day in, day out...and sometimes when the wind was right...Jelly had wanted to take his hunting rifle and puncture the piece of noisy shit with a large caliber hollow point…just explode the sorry device into another realm of hell.

But there it was, some poor cowboy crying out his sorry pain about the woman that done done him wrong. Now that Jelly was officially engaged to be married he figured these poor laments might start to make more sense. He almost laughed aloud and then he spotted the cruiser, lights out, engine on, exhaust purling from the rear pipes.

Jelly, dressed in dark clothes, pulled out his .38 pistol, flicked off the safety and slid over the fence and made it into the ditch off the side of the highway. In a few seconds of squat running he was behind the vehicle. One officer as far as he could see…in the driver's seat. He studied the wider area toward his house to see if there was someone on the dirt drive up to the front porch. Didn't see anything.

The officer rolled down the driver side window and lit a cigarette. The radio crackled with a call in Warden for the Southwest side of town. A break in. Jelly moved swiftly to the officer and slammed the hand flicking the cigarette down hard against the door. The cigarette went flying and he shoved his pistol against the neck of the patrol officer.

"Don't fuckin move, smart ass," Jelly said.

"Mi Dios!" cried a female and the tensed arm relaxed.

Jelly looked in the window and did a double-take. "Why Officer Gomez, what a surprise! Community outreach this time of night?"

"Mind taking that gun off me," she said.

"No problem," Jelly said. "I guess I can trust you if you start trusting me. Why am I under surveillance?"

"You tell me?" she said. "The Chief sent me out here."

"Yes, as back up to the drug bust sweeps tonight. Now why do you think you're watching me? Maybe a meth lab?"

"I'm not aware of anything like that. I just was told to watch your house and report if you made a move."

"A move where?"

"I don't know. Anywhere, I guess."

"Why don't you stop acting so innocent and tell me what I'm supposed to have done or might do."

"You're under suspicion for involvement with the drug gangs in the county, how's that?"

"You believe that?"

"I don't know. I just follow orders."

"You sure didn't like the way I treated Father Rodriguez today, did you?"

"No, you showed a real disrespect to that priest."

"Maybe my intuition was telling me something."

"Like what?"

"Like maybe he was just a little too cozy with Tito Santiago. Maybe I don't like men who hit their daughters in the face."

"That wasn't proven."

"Come on, officer, you saw the girl's face."

"That doesn't prove a thing."

"What does your gut tell you?"

"I was focused on the good will nature of our visit with the padre."

"I can see that. But maybe you have to open your eyes a little larger and take in more. Are you aware the padre has a twin brother involved with the Monterrey drug cartel?"

Wide-eyed, Officer Gomez stared at Jelly.

"Do you think that might compromise your actions as a priest?"

"I can't say. It wouldn't make it so, no."

"Are you being naïve just to irritate me, Officer Gomez?"

"No I am not!" she said hotly.

"You should be careful stalking around a farmhouse in the dark. You could have been shot just now."

"I haven't been stalking. I've been staked out here in the patrol car all this time."

Jelly looked at her and she stared back at him defiantly, her big brown eyes angry and focused.

"Then who the hell…" Jelly said and looked across the road and up the slight hill traversed by his drive and the old house and its windows glowing under the pecan trees. A swirl of gray smoke caught in the wind over the chimney and swept it skyward into the dark blue sky.

That's when the scream came from the farmhouse.

"That's Connie, my fiancée," Jelly said and ran around and jumped into the passenger side of the cruiser. "Let's go!"

They raced up the driveway and lurched to a stop near the front steps. Connie was outside on the porch. She was dressed in a sweatshirt, jeans and running shoes.

"I saw somebody at the kitchen window just now," she said. "A man's face."

Jelly grabbed a flashlight from the cruiser. "Stay here, Gomez," he said, "and cover the front of the house."

He circled the farmhouse, the flashlight working under the bushes and under the house elevated on brick pilings. He made a quick circuit of the house and then swept the nearby grove of trees. Nothing.

Gomez and Connie were talking in hushed tones when Jelly returned to the front porch. "Don't see anything, Connie. What did he look like?"

"He was kind of young but had wild looking hair sticking out the sides of his head. His eyes were huge, like an owl or something, but they looked crazy like fried eggs, you know the yolks were the center of his eyes...the pupils. Definitely some deranged character. Maybe an escapee from a drug rehab or mental hospital."

"Maybe a meth addict?" Gomez said.

Connie said, "Yes, he could have been. I was washing up the dishes and the light from the kitchen made it hard to see him at first but then when my eyes adjusted...oh my God, he was hovering right there in the frame of the window like a floating pumpkin head."

"Another version of the Ax Man legend," Gomez said. "I've been hearing about that guy from people all over the county."

"That can't be true," Connie said. "That boy has been dead for decades. It's just an old boogey man story."

Jelly's cell phone rang. Officer Gomez and Connie jumped.

"Yes?" Jelly said and heard a roar of cheering fans over the phone background.

Sammy's tenor voice broke through the mob noise. "Jelly?"

"Sammy, where are you?"

"At the high school stadium. Game's just over."

"Who won?"

"We did of course! The Cougars are leaving town with their tails between their legs. The Bobcats have a shot at the state championship."

"That's not why you called, is it?"

"Hell no..." Sammy said and went on to summarize what Celia had been saying about Bill and his weird behavior. "She's afraid he's mixed up with the local gangs."

"Which ones?"

"She has no idea. She wants me to drive her and the kids home but I'm thinking..."

"You're thinking right. Keep them over at your apartment until you hear from me. I'm going over to the farm right now and check it out."

"You sure you don't need some backup?" Sammy said, sounding like a gung ho rookie.

Jelly looked at Anna Gomez and Connie Sorensen standing on the top step of the porch…two tough professional women if he'd ever seen any. "No, I've got all the support I need."

CHAPTER 37

▼

Lou Ann Lovejoy didn't really like violence but when a heavy hand was needed, she knew how to deliver the blow. And that's exactly what she did to the handsome tanned cheek of one Jack Turner, sculptor and Don Juan of the bohemian realms of Atlanta and South Beach…the firm flat of her hand left a stinging red imprint.

Jack recoiled and drew back down the sofa out of reach of Lou Ann's fury.

"You sorry sonofabitch!" Lou Ann screamed. "You go fuckin' around on me and without protection and now you tell me you're on medication for herpes!"

"It's not that bad," Jack said and rubbed his face. He had long black hair and often had it coiled into Rasta fashion, cool with his Harley and his powerful weed he lazily doled out to friends. He had inherited an independent income from this mother's side of the family and he enjoyed the carefree life of the half-serious dharma bum. "Everything's cool. I got medication for it."

"But you haven't been taking it regular," Lou Ann said. "You fuckin' idiot. That can make it worse. It'll flare up like a wildfire."

"I'm doing all I can to keep you safe," Jack said and flashed his thick eyelashes over his sad green eyes.

God, what a hunk…but what a hunk of two timing bullshit! Lou Ann jumped up off the sofa and went to the bedroom where his bag lay. The top was unzipped but most of his clothes were still inside. He'd come down in a van with his latest construction tools to work on some found art pieces and pass the winter with her. That was history. Time for a strong message. Lou Ann took up the bag, heavier than she expected, and dragged it to the front door.

"What the hell are you doing?" Jack said and jumped up.

"I'm throwing your no good hide into the street," she said.

Jack grabbed the suitcase and they tussled over it. Lou Ann struggled and got out onto the front porch with her end and Jack came tumbling afterward. She snatched the handle and he lost his footing and rolled down the steps into the front yard.

Lou Ann laughed and pointed. "I'm so pissed off with you. You're lucky I don't drive down to my Daddy's house down yonder and get him up here with his shotgun. He'd take a leg off you, buster, that philandering middle leg."

Jack got to his feet. Lou Ann threw the bag at his feet.

"What about my other things," Jack said.

Lou Ann went back in and threw out his leather jacket and car keys. "And don't forget my brother's near here and he's on the Strickland police force, a detective, and he could have your ass for criminal negligence."

"Please, Lou Ann, I was gonna tell you, I just forgot in the moment of passion, you know how it is?"

"I know what passion is, Jack, you asshole! But I also know who's responsible for who? If you loved me, you wouldn't have put me at risk. You fuckin' jerk. If I get this goddamned disease, me and my family are coming lookin' for you, mister."

Jack mumbled something under his breath.

"Don't be talkin' back to me. You know you're guilty as sin. You rich asshole playboy. You don't give a shit about anybody but yourself. You're a fuckin' waste, you hear that. You're a no talent jerk!"

Jack's complexion turned bluish purple under his big jaw and two day beard. "And you're a dilettante without a prayer in the world."

"That's fine. Then we're two nobodies standing out here in the middle of the night screaming at each other. Just because you can't keep your dick in your pants don't mean I gotta suffer. I trusted you, Jack. You lied to me. You put me at risk. God knows I might have AIDS right now because of you."

"That's ridiculous," he said. "I said herpes not AIDS."

"Did you get tested for AIDS?"

Jack threw open the side door to his van and tossed his bag into the back.

"I ain't talkin' to you about nothing more," he said. "You can't handle the truth."

"I'd say you're mocking yourself, big shot. Gotta prove what a big man you are...probably fuckin' men down in South Beach."

He glared at Lou Ann. "Shut your trap, you bitch. I can come up there and kick your fat ass."

"Just try it, pretty boy," she said and stepped inside her front door.

Jack stood beside the van and shook his head. "Godammit, Lou Ann! Let's work something out…"

Lou Ann reappeared and waved a forty-five caliber pistol in his direction. "My Daddy give me this when I moved out here to the country. He said, honey, you never know what kind of trash blows into your yard but this thing will sure keep it flapping down the road."

"Oh, that's just great. Physical violence…how disappointing," Jack said and shook his head in disbelief. "Here it is nearly midnight and I been traveling all day to be with you…"

"And you were *with* me," Lou Ann said and cocked the gun, "and you lied to me about your STD…and you did so with criminal intent…"

"Unintended…"

"Bullshit," she said and brushed back her damp blonde hair. "Get off my property before I put a hole in that engine block and then another hole between your legs. You two timing gigolo."

"Rot in hell, Lou Ann Lovejoy, you hack artist!" Jack said and gave her a nasty, devilish grin. "I never loved your white trash ass. Fuck you."

"Fuck you too," Lou Ann said and aimed the pistol and squeezed off a thundering round.

The bullet blew a hole the size of a silver dollar through the windshield and clipped off his good luck medallion hanging from the mirror, his silver Harley miniature cycle.

"You're fuckin' nuts," he said and jumped in the van and started the engine.

"You're lucky to keep yours," Lou Ann said and laughed as he spun around her yard and bounced down the drive to the county two-lane. She watched until his red tail lights disappeared round the turn. Overhead a small plane droned over the clear cool sky. Lou Ann looked up and thought, wish I could escape up there and get out of this madness.

"Daddy…where you going this hour of the night?" Mama Lovejoy said.

He stood at the backdoor and cocked his head. "Thought I heard a gunshot."

"A what?" Mama called from the bedroom.

"Don't worry yourself, go on to bed," he said. "I'm getting some air."

"Now don't be long and don't be drinking out there."

"Mind your business, old woman," he muttered and found the pint bottle of whiskey in the empty flower pot.

He shoved out the back door and eased down the steps onto the grass of the backyard. Under the arbor trellis in the shadows cast by the security light, he undid the screw top and took a long swallow and felt the elixir sweep down his gullet and on to the burning joy of his stomach. He shook himself and thanked god he was drinkin' clean refined store bought whiskey. God almighty, no tellin' what white lightning moonshine would have done to him by now if he'd a gone on drinkin that crap. Moonshiners then, dope dealers now…just one damn thing after another…Federal boys just want their damned taxes…outta just legalize the shit…

He moved out into the yard and did a little turn by the mimosa tree. A van doing good speed came along the two-lane and failed to stop at the stop sign, just slowed and swerved right heading south. Some poor sonofabitch out chasing pussy on a damp Friday night. Poor dumb slob. It wasn't worth the trouble…just created more trouble.

He took another taste and thought about his great uncle Louis on his Daddy's side that got into trouble with a preacher's daughter…they was always loose as a goose…defying their Bible quoting daddies. And sure enough the slut got pregnant and wasn't real sure who the daddy was…so she finally picked great uncle Louis as her favorite and told all to her Daddy who of course got the sheriff after Louis…Hell, there weren't nothing to do, either marry the bitch or escape the county…and beyond.

So that's what old Louis did…He hightailed out of Strickland County and headed south, thumbing his way down into south Florida…down into the Everglades. This must've been back in the Twenties or maybe right before the Big War. And old Louis Lovejoy…by god he had to make some money and being a strapping mean sonofabitch, he took up gator wrestling at a tourist sideshow just outside of Coral Gables. Became the star attraction and saved his money and when things blew over back here he came home and got into the tobacco and cotton brokering business…Another boy had come forward as the father and married the preacher's daughter…a banker's son who went to Vanderbilt and afterwards got a nice job in a bank in Chattanooga.

A small plane circled over the fields and its engine seemed to change pitch like it was going to drop down and crop dust the field east of here. Daddy cocked his head and tried to hear it clear but his hearing was going like everything else. He sipped on the bottle and closed his eyes. Damn, but there had been plenty of traffic on the old side road up toward his farm this evening. Probably gonna drive Bill half insane, bunch of drunks blowing by his place.

"Daddy!" he heard the old woman cry out. "Get in here 'fore you catch your death."

He did a smart turnabout and saluted the distant drone of the plane. Fare thee well, lonely pilot, he mused, too bad you can't stay up there above all this human trouble down here. Hell's bells...he was a weary old man come to nothing much at all. He took the now empty pint bottle and slung it through the night toward his tool shed. It disappeared with a splintering crunch...

"Another dead soldier," he said and spat after it. "God bless now."

CHAPTER 38

▼

Tito Santiago had a nervous habit, a little tic over his right eyebrow, where once a blade had flashed in a dark alley in Nuevo Laredo and almost lost his eye. The man died who did that to him, the puta, the whore. But ever since that attack, that scar and its healing, gracias a Dios, was a signal for the good or ill of things to come.

As he stood in the dark copse of trees, separating the back field from the front of this gringo, Bill Lovejoy, he looked up at the dark sky and felt a slight tremor along the scar line. Something that could blind you, a knife or things gone bad. It was just this sense of things, this slight imbalance, that a life hung on.

Yes, he needed new airfields all the time and yes it was time to light the flares along the corners, to outline the landing strip, but it wasn't anything but this damned scar on his eye, this shadow of his own death that mattered. That was his good luck and he stared at the stars, the rain gone for a change, and knew this was his destino…a man of knowing. That was why he was here in this God forsaken American wilderness of rednecks and blacks…campesinos spreading across America, cleaning toilets, vacuuming carpets in big glass towers night and day, doing the shit work of the white men, or cleaning their homes for their pampered white wives, or playing nanny to the little children…

And out here in the countryside, where these southern people with their black slaves now a so-called free people, with the boot on their necks and their Walmart jobs…it was a joke. La Raza was back…from Florida to California and north into Canada. You could feel the change like the undertow at a beach, pulling you into places of power and wealth. Only a matter of time and he was with these others in his gang the front line of this invasion. These people did not know the desperate drive of his bosses, of the lines of communication stretching all the way back into old Mexico and its ruthless history of blood and sacrifice. He felt his eyebrow twitch with the thought of blood sacrifice and saw for a second the Aztec priest driving the sacrificial knife into the heart of his victim…a beating heart held aloft to feed an insatiable hunger of a sun god without remorse. His grandmother had taught him about that blood thirst and had shown him how the Catholic priests were doing the same…everywhere, sacrifice and blood. Without that resolve, a man was not a man.

Above him he heard the drone of the plane and then he spotted its red and green wing lights wavering like a slow bird flapping over the dark fringe of forest that ran along the Sandy Creek. There were several dirt road exits through the back of the property, just in case, and this man Bill Lovejoy seemed to be an odd man who practiced the severe look of a hard man but Tito smiled and knew this was a man who had spent too long in his own haunts, a man without a big heart, a lonely man who needed the danger to bring his life back to him. All this and the risk of his family and fortune, just to work with the changes coming over this county. Inevitable but sad to see a man so outside the course of things that he was a traitor to his own people and had to trust extranjeros. Trust was the thing. Loyalty. And this Bill, this tall man with his somber ways, Tito knew men and knew this was a man damaged in his soul…susto, soul loss. But when it came to building out into alliances, you took the misfits first and dealt with the consequences. If there were loose ends, they were snipped off. The lust of drugs, the river of money, it never stopped, and only the people changed.

"Jefe, tiempo por el fuego," Juan shouted. Time to light the flares?

Tito took a final look around the dark grove of trees. The pick up truck and van were ready. His men were armed. And off there by the road leading back to the farmhouse was Bill Lovejoy with Hector and Manuel, well-armed, expert with pistols and knives. Pity the poor gringo who betrayed him. Pity any soul who took up arms against this cartel. Look what his sharpshooters had already done to the rednecks in their stupid meth truck labs. One by one, we would erase these competitors. One by one, the local power nobodies would sign up and take their morditas, their little bites out of the body of money, their blood money. Tito remembered squeezing the trigger on the judge in Texas as he stood tall against the cartel, smug that he had his pigeon in the country jail and that he had cracked the great silent barrier. That slow steady squeeze…the jerk of the rifle, the explosion of the judge's soft fluffy red brains, like a cloud of scrambled eggs, splattering against the windshield of his car. Asesino! The papers cried from San

Antonio to Juarez…In your gut you had to know when it was time and that time was now…

"Fuego!" Tito commanded.

And along the back field, the men lit up the flares at the four corners and midway along the air strip.

"Jefe," Juan said with a lively smile, "esta noche, dos cosas del cielo, eh, dios y drogas?"

"Sí," Tito said, "tonight, two things from the heavens, god and drugs."

The twin engine plane dipped, disappeared for a second or two, then reappeared as if resurrected from the Sandy Creek's dark waters and lights out, engines feathered, coasted down the air strip and touched down on the hay strewn field.

CHAPTER 39

▼

In his pickup Jelly had his two female companions, Connie in the middle and Gomez by the window. Gomez wouldn't stay with her car if he left, nor would he allow her to tag along with a marked police car since that would blow the element of surprise for the DET gang.

"You do what I say," Jelly said to Gomez. "And bring the night vision binoculars."

They had two shotguns and each of them wore a pistol. Connie knew how to shoot, he'd taught her at the range and some target practice down in the woods. But he didn't intend to have either of them in the line of fire. In fact as he headed up the road to Bill's farm, or what was always in everyone's mind, the Lovejoy place...he didn't have a definite plan and so was going in on instinct. Actually that made him more alert and comfortable than having a definite approach to extracting Bill from a stupid and very possibly deadly situation.

At some level he hated his older brother, just as he hated his father, because in so many ways they were the same in their treatment of other family members...my way or the highway. Authoritarian assholes. You couldn't tell him a damned thing; and when they saw the error of their ways, they had the hardest time admitting it. He'd struggled with his feelings toward both of them for years. And finally, one day not long after confessing his feelings of sibling and paternal hatred to Connie, and listening to her thoughts (women were amazing about people and relationships, far superior to men...it was so stunningly obvious)...he'd gone through a kind of shift. He'd finally said, oh, so this is the way it is.

And the way it was that the top kicks in the family, the patriarch of the farm and all its wealth making, all that benefit came at a cost to him and his mother and siblings. Because he saw it at last that his father and brother had a goddamned chip on their shoulders. They were sacrificing for all of the others, suffering the Old Testament pains of farmer saviors. They suffered and so everyone dependent on them, needed, nay, deserved to suffer to make up for that imbalance. And for Bill, and less so for his Daddy, Jelly had come to realize that Bill hated him for his existence, and that was considered a fair price for being in the family. Bill got his way without question and the denial of Jelly's life or its value was a given. In fact as he reflected over these dark issues of sibling anger, this denial was a kind of death, a kind of psychic murder that was justified inside and underneath the family's picture of things. Bill despised Sammy for his literacy and city job. He hated Lou Ann for her useless art career. He'd written Ella off years ago for being an airhead mystic who married up into a richer, bigger farm family. Three kids and managing a home didn't seem to register. That was much the way he treated Celia his wife, who never felt good enough. Then Bill hated Jelly for his sympathy for the poor and the misguided, and most of all because he got a government check as a policeman…as if farmers didn't know how to milk the government for support.

But Jelly had talked to Connie at length, going into it, not wanting the feelings and understandings to go away. And she had said at one point, sipping a brandy on the porch one spring night, "Fathers are such tragedies…oldest big brothers too." And Jelly had jumped on that and wondered why that was the case, and she had answered in a reverie, "Because they try to make and enforce the rules. They're doomed to failure."

On another occasion she remarked that Bill's simmering anger reminded her of the Biblical conflict of Cain and Able. Cain the agriculturalist, Able the pastoralist with his gentle sheep herding. And the fact that he Jelly was the youngest, the "baby" of the family, had no doubt angered Bill with jealousy.

"But I'm not a sheep herder," Jelly objected.

And Connie had smiled and said, "What's a public safety officer but a guy who herds the mob around and keeps them on the straight and narrow."

Jelly looked over now at Connie who glanced back at him. She looked pale in the light of the reflected headlights and the control panel. He patted her on the leg to reassure her. They had reached the dirt road turn off toward Bill's. From here on the road went on past the house.

"Okay, when I give the signal I want you two to sink below window level. We're going to cruise by the front gate of the farm to see what's what from a distance. Lay the shotguns on the floor."

"We need to be aware of the DET plans," Gomez cautioned. "We don't want to trip up their plans."

"I intend to extract my brother if possible before any violence begins," Jelly said.

"Sir, I have issues with this," Gomez said.

Jelly came to a full stop. "You can get out here, Gomez. But don't call in any info on me. You'll just set us up."

Gomez took the handle of the door and began to open it. "I don't know where the DET team is."

"No you don't and you might just walk up on them and be a victim of so-called friendly fire. That gunfire would warn the drug dealers…if in fact they're out here tonight."

Gomez looked confused.

"Look, you decided to come along to keep that loose cannon Lovejoy under surveillance. And I agreed to it. You can be our backup."

"All right," Gomez said and let out a gasp. "You've been nothing but trouble for me all day. I can't believe I'm here."

"Believe it," Connie said. "I do and I just got engaged."

"You poor thing," Gomez said and looked at us both.

Jelly and Connie both laughed.

Jelly said, "Thanks, Gomez, now I know I did the right thing."

Near Bill's farmhouse Jelly gave the sign for the women to drop down. Jelly wore his jean jacket and his faded green John Deere baseball cap…just a good old boy. He slowed down and coasted by Bill's.

At first he didn't see anyone but by the gate, not to his surprise, he spotted a pickup, not Bill's…and two guys, Mexicans standing in the shadows. They watched him as he passed slowly by and he gave them a friendly wave. They nodded and returned the wave. Yep, just get along and move along…

The trees along the culvert intervened now.

"What'd you see?" Connie said.

"Stay down," Jelly said. I'm coming to another gate."

Here was the old pasture fence and an old gate seldom used. Jelly knew all the entries, every inch of the old property, having grown up on it and having been pressed into service, mostly involuntary all his years growing up, whether it was cattle, or tobacco, sorghum, cabbage or cotton, watermelon or peanuts…it didn't matter what they tried, it was all hard work and he'd done his part over the years. He shut down the lights and pulled up to the pasture entrance.

"Okay, Gomez," Jelly said, scanning the area with the infrared binoculars. "It looks all clear. Open the latch on the right there…and leave it open after I pull through. We may need to come back this way and in a hurry."

The women sat up and Gomez got out and undid the fence and swung it open. It creaked and Jelly winced. He pulled his pistol and flipped off the safety and opened his window in case he needed a shot. Gomez returned to the cab of the truck and slid in…

Jelly eased through the gate and started up the pasture road, lights off…and then came to a stop. "You hear that?"

"Over there," Connie said, pointing east. "There was a plane drifting low over the trees ahead and its lights swung up and down, one wing tipping in a salute, then the other.

Jelly accelerated up the road, smoothly, steadily, remembering the road in his memory, glancing through the binoculars.

Then they all saw the lights to the right.

"Landing lights," Gomez said. "It's gotta be the Mexican cartel. If anything goes wrong, you know they'll blame your brother."

"You got it, Gomez…my brother Bill is in one deep well of shit," Jelly said and sped up, lurching through a pothole. "Hold on, troops."

They reached a rise and pulled up behind a copse of long standing pine trees. The plane was taxiing toward a group of men standing under the trees by the last curing barn on the old farm. Jelly scanned the group and spotted Bill's lanky frame and Tito and the other Mexicans around him. They were focused on the airplane which had flashed its landing lights as it rolled to a stop. The men advanced on foot toward the plane and a pickup and a van appeared from behind the curing barn and followed them toward the plane.

Gomez whispered, "Where's the DET?"

"I'm wondering the same thing," Jelly said and focused the binoculars on the fringe of woods along Sandy Creek, the only other option for them unless they planned to bust in the front gate…and that would just forewarn Tito and his gang…

"The Chief wanted to lead this one," Gomez said.

"Well that explains the pace of things," Jelly said.

"I've got a bad feeling about this," Connie said and clutched Jelly's arm.

"Timing's everything," Jelly whispered back, wondering what the hell he was going to do.

CHAPTER 40

───────── ▼ ─────────

Bill Lovejoy wasn't comfortable with these Mexicans. He was deep into it now and there was no turning back…well not now. But he knew a bad vibe when he got to a place that had gone wrong. He was in limbo now somewhere between his idealistic furor over the impoverishment of the small farmer and this gritty group of gangsters…for that's what they were as he listened to them in their Spanish, their darting eyes, the flash of smiles and the grim looks.

Bill was armed with a pistol on his hip but that really meant nothing, surrounded by these men who in another place looked like hard carnival workers, men who had seen cruelty and had grown accustomed to its face. It was their road and life was hard and cheap. This brutal edge had only gradually sunk into his smug pride of civil disobedience. Whereas his protest was an act of desperate refusal, untrained, these men were living this dual life of gangster and fieldworker for real.

Tito Santiago was a treacherous individual. He could see that. But he had hoped that being only in the distribution pipeline might be just enough to play along in the underground market and when these guys grew tired of his farm as a safe point, they'd move on to the next farmer. This evening with Tito and his men convinced himself he couldn't keep this level of tension going with his family kept at bay. Too, he knew, had always known, although stupidly denying it, that those who crossed these characters often lost not only their own lives but all related family members. It was the price for betrayal.

Seeing the plane make the landing, Tito clapped his hands and said something quickly in Spanish to his men who began to move toward the plane. He looked at Bill and smiled.

"Good job, Bill," he said. "That hay you put down. That was good. Look, the plane didn't sink in the mud."

"There's good drainage back here," Bill said again for the umpteenth time. "Down to the Sandy Creek."

This guy Tito was a fanatic for detail. He seemed to be hyper-aware of every problem. But then he was the jefe, the chief, and that role and respect had to be earned the hard way. Tito had talked at length to Bill about his brother Jelly on the police force. Bill had finally seemed to convince him that Jelly was, yes, a brother, but a brother from another world, a world he didn't agree to.

"We are enemies on most things," Bill finally said. "We don't talk much."

"It's the same in Mexico sometimes," Tito had said and seemed satisfied. "Hermanos are sometimes the worst of enemies."

And tonight Tito had pulled him aside and whispered, "It's a good thing, Bill, that your hermano is a good enemy. Today I meet him in town face to face and he is no soft man even with this name of fruit jelly."

The van and truck pulled next to the plane. Bill walked toward the plane with Tito and his lieutenant Luis. Tito's men were already emptying packages into the van, moving quickly and efficiently. They weren't rookies. Some of this stuff they might decide to keep in his curing barns, underground in sealed lockers…but Bill hadn't encouraged this notion. He had made it clear that he wanted to provide a private airfield as a first step. Tito had smiled and stared at him for a moment.

"Want to go slow, eh?" he said.

"That's the size of it," Bill had said.

"That's smart," Tito said. "We want lots of landing opportunities."

Bill had negotiated for a one-time landing rights fee of $15,000 cash upon arrival of the first plane…payment due in a few minutes as he saw it. He swallowed and felt sweat trickle down his armpits. His hands were damp and he felt slightly sick to his stomach. He tried to blot out his uncertain picture of Celia and the kids being parked in town until the all clear. Just stay focused, he repeated to himself…

And then Bill felt the world shift under his feet. The passenger door swung open and Tito greeted a man dressed in a priest's habit and white collar. They gave each other a full hug and back slap. They laughed and spoke in Spanish he had no way of grasping. Tito helped him down and Luis grabbed his suitcase. The priest took a quick glance at Bill. Tito escorted the priest to the truck and helped him in while Luis stowed his bag.

"Who's that?" Bill wanted to know when Tito returned.

"Oh that's a padre, a friend of mine. I'm giving him a faster ride to his parish…than you know, on the goddamned bus or driving here from Texas. You can forget you saw him."

"You never said anything about transporting people."

Tito smiled. "It's like we say, god and gold, it all comes to the same thing."

"How's that the same?" Bill said,

Tito smiled and looked at Bill like he was an annoying horsefly. "We only take a minute now. Calmo, señor."

Bill almost said something about the money but waited, trying to keep his poker face.

Tito yelled at his men and they hurried and slammed the doors shut on the van. There were packages wrapped in foil with heavy tape. Water resistant. He didn't know what kind of drugs they were bringing in and didn't want to know. The sample of grass he'd been given last week by Tito was proof enough that he dealt in a good product. Bill had begun to enjoy the smoking…late at night, walking the back fields, an excellent companion, despite his paranoid feelings.

The truck and van pulled away from the plane and moved toward the road to the farmhouse and stopped. Tito waved his arms over his head and the pilot revved one engine of the Cessna and turned the plane around slowly at the end of the strip until it faced the full length of the runway. Tito ran up to the pilot and yelled something and slapped the side of the plane farewell. The pilot revved both engines now and Bill and Tito and Luis stood in the wind behind the propellers.

"The pilot says you do good job on the landing," Tito said. "Very firm after all this rain."

"Great," Bill said and gave a grinning Tito and Luis a thumb up.

The plane shuddered and then began to roll forward slowly…

CHAPTER 41

▼

Jelly knew his brother's slouching habits. He knew a beaten man. He could see Bill was walking toward his death and he knew for a pure instant, staring through the windshield of his truck, that Bill knew it too.

"They're gonna let the plane take off and get away," Gomez said. "Where's the DET?"

Jelly said, "They're gonna hit Tito and his gang down by the gate or after they leave the farm...we need an attack now."

"See that priest that got out of the plane," Connie said. "What's that all about?"

Gomez' eyes met Jelly's in a glance. Yes, the evil twin had arrived and was going underground at the local parish. Gomez shook her head in disbelief.

"Let's say that new rectory addition in town requires a new priest...all compliments of the familia Santiago," Jelly said.

"They're buying a priest?" Connie said.

"I'll explain later, listen..." Jelly said and looked at the two women. "Bill's up the creek and I've got to break up this party."

Connie looked stunned. "What are you going to do?"

Jelly wasn't sure. Pull a magic rabbit out of my hat, he wanted to joke, but he sensed he had no time and he didn't feel like joking. He had to create a diversion.

"Both of you out of the truck. Take cover behind the tree line here and when all hell breaks loose, I want you to lay down a line of fire at the gang and trucks. Gomez, try to reach the Chief...we need backup now."

They both stared at him. "Are you crazy?" Connie said.

"Do it, now, out, please!" Jelly said. "Take the shotguns and Connie stay with Gomez! Go!"

They slid out of the truck. Connie leaned in the open window.

"Jelly Lovejoy, you better not get yourself killed, not after you've proposed…"

"What are you going to do?"

"I'll have to kill you," she said matter of factly.

"Noted, my dear, you're marrying a cop…stay low…until the DET sweeps in."

The women dropped to a crouch in the pines. Jelly spotted Luis pulling his revolver and falling in behind Bill. Not good…

Lights out on the truck, Jelly gunned it out of the trees and accelerated across the back field. He drove straight at Tito and his gang who stood watching the plane…At last they seemed to grasp the situation and turned as if in slow motion and faced his truck, while drawing their weapons and taking aim…

Jelly ducked down and heard the glass shatter over his head and as he passed them he heard their shouts in Spanish.

"Pendejo!"

Dickhead…whatever else, he didn't know and he swerved the truck as bullets plonked into the frame and then he raised up enough to aim the truck right into the plane where the right wing met the fuselage. He threw open the door and jumped…into an eerie night flight of his own that seemed to take far longer than reality required…

Hitting the field of mud and clay knocked his breath from his chest and he gasped as a blinding flash of pain drove up his side. The truck smashed into the plane and blew a sickening metallic, hollow explosion through the fuselage. There was a rip of light and a flume of fuel and fire streaming down the wing. The plane rolled a few feet in a short arc and jerked to a stop. Jelly tried to get up and couldn't…something was wrong with his leg…It felt dislocated. He unsnapped his pistol on his hip and pointed it in the direction of the plane. The pilot shoved open the cockpit door and jumped to the ground and started running across the field away from him. The pilot tripped and fell and got up again, stumbling.

Jelly heard small arm fire and heard rounds whistling over his head and slapping into the dirt around him. He twisted over and saw Bill backing into the thick old locust trees dividing the front fields from the back. Luis, Tito's lieutenant, fired his gun repeatedly after Bill. Jelly got off a shot and knocked Luis to the ground. The priest pulled out a weapon and Bill shot him. Jelly saw flashes of gunfire from the pine trees where he left Gomez and Connie. The drug van and truck were in motion heading out of the back field toward the front road…Bill went after them, firing his pistol. The narcotraficantes were firing with automatic weapons, raking the woods and field near the burning plane.

Jelly heard distant gunfire toward Bill's farmhouse…the DET…must be there at the front gate. He tried to get to his feet and managed to get up on one knee when he saw a boot meet his face and catch him in the jaw. Jelly saw Tito Santiago's leering face as he went down hard on his back. Above him were the stars…a clear sky at last…Jelly thought in a kind of spacey detachment. But the stars were blotted out by the rageful, hard face of Tito Santiago who stared down at him like a new constellation…the Mexican jefe…

"You and your brother are dead men, gelatina! All your family dies now too!"

Jelly lay there on the cold wet ground and saw the pistol swing over his face like an executioner's pendulum. He tried to raise his outstretched arms toward the barrel of the pistol but his strength was gone and the pain in his leg was too much to support him. Jelly saw Tito's eye twitch and he heard the trigger click and a flare of fire like a roman candle hit Jelly's face, an intense heat hit his skin and his body jerked…there was a roar like hell itself had opened and then there was nothing…no light, no stars, no sound…just a vast nothing. Jelly felt himself smiling, relieved of all human duties, off duty at long last from his human family. Like a phone line buzzing with static, at last the nervous electricity dissolved into a profound silence.

CHAPTER 42

▼

Far across Strickland County Dahlia lay on her bed and propped up by two fluffy pillows. Her heart ached and she felt an emptiness in her flesh, as if she were slowly being erased by some force beyond her awareness. The rain had stopped some time ago. Ella had visited her within the past hour and treated her with medicines and with a cool wash cloth had stroked her parched face.

Dahlia liked those old rainy days when she was growing up on the Lovejoy farm…From somewhere betwixt here and there, between something and nothing, she remembered a day like a playing card slipped from the deck of her dream of the Lovejoys. Hangin' round with Ella way back when they were teen girls, almost full grown young women…

Yes, Lord, rainin' hard…and over at the Lovejoys, Lou Ann's been cryin', Sammy's been whinin', Ella's been bitchin' and Lord God Almighty, here come Grandma Rose with a bouquet of forget-me-nots and she's sure singin' the blues. Bill's skinned his knee nearly raw to the bone, the cat Ossie's screechin' at the screen door, and Mama's got on her martyr's hang dog face. Daddy's cursin' that old Ford in the backyard, tore his knuckles freein' up that cracked distributor cap, and the ten year old baby…Jelly, he's yellin' shut up, can't hear the TV above all this piss'n' and moanin', liable, he threatens, to go out to the barn and shoot hisself to get some peace and quiet, with nobody round to bother nobody, no time to worry 'bout, and is anybody goin' to town to get groceries and mail, 'cause the truck needs gas and Sandra up at the Safeway wants her reading glasses, she's already called twice this mornin'. Lord, she's persistent like all them Flags, ornery you get'em on the wrong side of the bed or the law, so don't forget her damned glasses, they're down the hall on the table by the front door, and by the way, Miss Smarty Pants Lou Ann's bra's hangin' on the staircase railin'—or like she likes to say, *newel post*...and look it on the tube—there's been another snot nose teen shootin' his daddy's gun at school, woundin' teachers and students...nobody killed, Jelly announces, and so nobody goes in to see the latest bloodshed, 'cause Daddy and Mama's goin' at it Big Time, and Granny Rose dropped her vase of forget-me-nots, and she's bellowin' with Lou Ann like sick cows, and there goes Bill moanin' and takin' on 'bout his knee and Ossie's got her tail caught in the screen do' and it still rainin' to beat hell! Lord have mercy on the Lovejoys...Dahlia prayed.

CHAPTER 43

▼

Granny Rose sat up in her bed in the back room of her trailer and cocked her head.

"Lord, sounds like the Civil War out there. Just listen to them guns going off. I wonder if Sam's got himself into trouble again with the neighbors over that piece of swamp land. Lord, what those men won't do to fight over something…"

She squinted into the gloomy light of the narrow hallway and heard a jolt in the trailer bed. Why, that's the front door coming loose, I reckon…

"Who's there? You might have the courtesy to knock once and a while."

There was a heavy step and a dragging sound, another heavy step and a dragging sound…

"Sam! What's happening out there? You hear all that shooting?"

A tall young man, his hair wild, his eyes like scrambled eggs peered in the doorway at her. He was dragging an ax behind him and she was sure, if her old eyes weren't lying to her that there was blood on it. Oh Lord, she prayed, cut me a little slack…

"You're not Sam," she managed.

"No ma'am," the boy's voice came to her, wavy like through water. "It's Tommy Edwards."

"Tommy Edwards," Granny Rose said and her throat went dry and she couldn't swallow and her next few words died in her mouth.

They stared at each other. He slumped forward and eased down on a chair covered in her day clothes.

"Have to excuse this mess, Tommy," she said. "I don't generally have visitors back here."

"I don't mind," he said and hung his head and stared at her. "I've seen just about everything."

"I reckon you have...You been hearing all that shootin'?"

"I have...ma'am...hearin' and seein'...all over this county."

"You might as well be straight with an old woman like me, Tommy, but have you come for me tonight..."

He looked at her a long time and at last gave her a weary smile. "No ma'am, I've had enough for now...I'm goin' away for a while."

Granny Rose nodded. "Filled up that appetite of yours, have you?"

He nodded.

"Well I'm glad you come by to see me 'fore you go back down yonder...to the lime sink, ain't that right?"

"Yes ma'am, back to the lime sink and my quiet resting place."

"Your home...every soul's gotta have a home, ain't that right?"

"Yes, ma'am."

"Did I ever finish reading those love letters from my beau Paul?"

"No, I don't think so...he said he was coming over to see you and then he didn't come, did he?"

Granny Rose hung her head and picked at the bed spread. "No, he never came, Tommy. That was his last letter. He come down with that swine flu back that was spreading around in '18...they sent him home from the training camp...and the folks wouldn't let us get together...so I sneaked off on the plow horse and rode half the night to his folks' house...and there he was, fever burning him up, him sweating and swearing and hardly knowing who was who...his folks let me stay with him all that night and I washed his sad face with cold water but there was nothing that could be done for poor Paul...In the morning the dear Lord took him up on the silvery wings, Tommy...for surely he was an angel..."

"Ahhhhgggg..." gurgled Tommy Edwards, alias the Ax Man, and he bent forward and hung his face staring at the floor.

"Now don't you fret none," Granny Rose said. "You get to my age you don't much care anymore. Your day will come, Tommy. Jesus will come for you...he's coming back for all of us, hon."

Granny Rose pulled back the curtains of her bedroom window and watched the tall figure, slumping like a beaten soul, dragging himself off into the dim light of the live oaks with the bearded moss hanging down like old men watching over the land below. Back to the lime sink and the black river waters. She shook her head in despair. Lord, Lord, she mused, life's one long row to hoe, now ain't it?

She licked her lips and puckered up her toothless, cratered mouth…wonder if that Jelly's gonna bring me some more boiled peanuts today?

EPILOGUE

▼

Sammy did his best to keep up the running narrative of the Lovejoy family history. It wasn't easy what with all the other loose ends fraying in an every increasingly chaotic world. He couldn't find a voice for the book and he couldn't think of a proper structure. Historical-minded people advised him to keep it simple and chronological, old to new, but something in his stubborn nature kept him mulling the storytelling over like a cow's cud.

What he did do was keep telegraphic notes on ongoing events.

When it came to the big farm shootout chapter he tried to piece it all together like a puzzle of newspaper clippings. Like a blast from a shotgun, there were a lot of fragments but they tended to have a kind of pattern...some places the pellets struck and right next to that might be a sizeable space where luck and mathematics of trajectory freed the receiver a heap of physical and psychic pain. This kind of thinking was just the very reason he would never finish this family history book. Still, he tried getting the notes down and maybe one day another Lovejoy might find the task quite easy...although he or she would have no nerve endings.

First of all, at the big shootout, remarkably no one died. Plenty of people were wounded, some traumatically, but that mathematical luck, that askew-ness of trajectory and fate, wounded but did not kill a single participant in the Lovejoy Farm shootout. *The Atlanta Constitution* wrote one wry article that referred to it as the cops and cartel that couldn't shoot straight.

Tito Santiago tried to kill Jelly with a direct shot to the head. But one Connie Sorensen, advancing like a banshee warrior with female wrath unleashed, was not going to have her future husband blown away. She came to a full stop, halfway across the field, took aim with the shotgun and squeezed off the twelve gauge.

Tito's infamous eye twitch gave off the fateful signal of incoming death and he flinched as he fired into the head of Jelly Lovejoy, supposedly an off duty and vacationing cop (more to follow). The bullet grazed and chipped his skull, knocking him unconscious into a twelve hour coma. He awoke with the Lovejoy clan surrounding him and Connie. The hospital floor was filled with angry men in pain, many under guard. Tito underwent surgery to save the eye; plastic surgery repaired his face and he recovered in prison, along with his wounded henchmen. Luis and the fake priest were wounded, seriously in the case of the twin of the real priest with a gut wound. Two other Mexicans and a DET member suffered minor wounds. Officer Gomez got a cut on her cheek running through the trees, chasing down the runaway pilot. Bill was unharmed and needed no medical attention in his jail cell at the county correctional facility. Naturally he wasn't at Jelly's bedside when he came to.

Sammy was there with the rest of the clan to welcome him back. There was a great cheer.

Jelly's first words were: "Is this heaven or hell?"

Granny Rose said without a hitch, "Some where's between, I reckon."

There wasn't a dry eye.

What else, Sammy wondered, needed to be said…well, plenty really but that was getting on to other future chapters maybe.

Jelly and Connie were married the next month in December. Connie said, "I'm taking no chances."

Jelly quit the police force and went to law school the next spring up at the University of Georgia in Athens, starting out of sequence…but he said, it didn't matter, he'd always done things slowly and backwards. He was a changed man…and laughing again…like he was back when…before the incident…but that's already been covered.

Sammy reviewed the notes.

Oh, and Bill of course did a stint in the big house, a little over two years. When he got out he sold the farm to a suburban home developer and he and Celia split up the money and the marriage. Bill's living in California and going through some changes, as he puts it; Celia's living in town in a nice new home, and well, she and the family historian, ahem, are working through their own support issues and quite pleasantly so…But that's a matter for another chapter. Tanya and Jay are getting along fine.

As far as that goes, the Lovejoys have hit a good patch for a while and everyone's trying to hold their mouth just the right way and keep the magic alive. Granny Rose says the Ax Man's gone down under for a spell; the blacks in town agree with her. The Mexicans haven't been around long enough to believe in Tommy Edwards; they've got their own bag of trouble. Even Dahlia's making a comeback from her leukemia and she's saying Ella's nightly hot toddy of brandy and bourbon and sugar have a lot to do with that…she's swearing by it. Now that they're drinking more, Ella's husband is drinking less and liking it…so does the rest of the family. Ella's also tending a little confidential patch of curative herb in the kitchen garden that has been most supportive of Dahlia's asthma and general nausea.

And of course, Sammy stretched out his notes, Mama's still keeping faith with the Bible and a yardarm of vitamin pills. Daddy's keeping the faith with his faithful pocket pints and his solo trips to town for franchise food. He said not long ago, that's the likely source of all the paper trash along the county highways (a frequent editorial complaint by the lady folk of the region)…was due to old farmers tossing out their sinful hamburger and fries paper to escape the wrath of their home-cooking jailers. Wink wink.

Then as for Granny Rose…well, what's to tell…she's been wandering the highways again bagging road cabbages (dropped off trucks usually at turns in the road). You'd think she was East European or something. She claims cabbage keeps her head on straight and bugs from biting. "What the hell more you want," she said recently at dinner.

Lou Ann's getting serious with a Savannah art dealer. There's talk of an engagement. He's got a townhouse and beach cabin at Tybee Island. Lou Ann's been staying at the beach place to paint.

Officer Anna Gomez was promoted and now helps out in a poverty law outreach program that tries to help kids stay in school. The real Father Rodriguez was reassigned to a Diocese in New Mexico; his evil twin was extradited after considerable wrangling back to Mexican authorities.

Chief Eldridge retired soon after the Lovejoy Farm Shootout. He said in his resignation, "I've seen too much and don't care how things turn out anymore. Shoot first, ask questions later…might have been the fairest police policy after all."

Al Morris, Jelly's partner, turned down the job in Flagstaff, Arizona, was promoted to Head of Detectives for Strickland County and is the leading candidate to replace Eldridge.

Well, what else for this slice of the family history, Sammy mused…Jelly and Connie are coming back to Strickland after law school and Jelly is going to start out as a public defender at the courthouse. They're planning on starting a family then. For now Buzz the cat is still the center of attention, a very spoiled working cat.

Guess that's about it, Sammy pondered and made a doodle bug shape. Oh, and Tanya and Jay wanted him to end this chapter in the ancient ledger book with the little ditty he taught them when they go fishing on weekends.

So, Sammy scribbled, here's to the joyful madness of youth and love:

> Have you ever been a fishin'
> On a hot summer's day
> Sit on the back and watch the fishes play
> With your hands in your pockets
> And your pockets in your pants
> And watch the little fishes
> Do the hootchy-kootchy dance.

The End

978-0-595-36363-6
0-595-36363-6

Printed in the United States
37838LVS00005B/12